Essie Rose's Revelation Summer

To President and Mrs.
Carter

Deanie Yasner

In gratitude
and
In Peace

Deanie

(ᕎ) **Golden Alley Press**
Emmaus, Pennsylvania

Golden Alley Press
37 S. Sixth Street
Emmaus, Pennsylvania 18049

www.goldenalleypress.com

The text of this book is set in Adobe Caslon
Book design by Michael Sayre

Printed in the United States of America

Publisher's Cataloging-in-Publication Data
Names: Yasner, Deanie, 1942- author.
Title: Essie Rose's revelation summer / Deanie Yasner.
Description: Emmaus, PA : Golden Alley Press, 2019. | Summary: In 1953, the lone Jewish girl in a small Mississippi town publicly challenges segregation. | Audience: Grades 3-6.
Identifiers: LCCN 2019946027 (print) | ISBN 978-1-7320276-9-5 (paperback) | ISBN 978-1-7333055-0-1 (ebook)
Subjects: LCSH: Racism--Juvenile fiction. | CYAC: Racism--Fiction. | Segregation--Fiction. | Jews--Fiction. | Friendship--Fiction. | Determination (Personality trait)--Fiction. | BISAC: JUVENILE FICTION / Social Themes / Prejudice & Racism. | JUVENILE FICTION / Diversity & Multicultural. | JUVENILE FICTION / Social Themes / Friendship. | JUVENILE FICTION / Girls & Women.
Classification: LCC PZ7.1.Y376 Es 2019 (print) | LCC PZ7.1.Y376 (ebook) | DDC [Fic]--dc23.

Front cover art: Michael Sayre
Photograph of the author: © Carol Ross

10 9 8 7 6 5 4 3 2

To Delphia, my real Pearlie May

and

To Esther Hershenhorn

Beth had to stay off her ankle, which is how she and I wound up in the lodge, playing Scrabble and reading books about failed expeditions; we sat in rocking chairs, very close to the windows that watched the mountains. Beth's book was about explorers who landed in one place but believed they were in another; my book was about men trying to find the Northwest Passage. Beth read aloud to me from her book, which said that Christopher Columbus visited Haiti and several Caribbean islands, but returned to Europe convinced he had discovered the coast of China. On a voyage to discover the Indian Ocean, he landed in Central America.

"He was a geographical idiot, Hazel." Beth stood on one leg and hopped over to warm herself in front of the fire. "He sailed anywhere at all, then said he'd arrived at his intended destination."

"Maybe all places were the same to him," I said.

"Then why was he an explorer?" Beth shut the book.

"In my book, New York was discovered because this guy, Henry Hudson, was looking for the North-west Passage," I said.

"Did he find the passage?"

"No," I said, "just New York."

I convinced my family to go to a party at the lodge on our last evening. We made up fake facts about ourselves and spent one night pretending to be Bighorns.

"Hi, I'm Harry Bighorn," our father said to the first strangers we met and Beth and I could barely contain our laughter. Our mother stood beside our father, beaming; she pretended that she loved to ski.

"I'm wild about algebra," I told an old woman who asked about my favorite subject in school.

"Me too," Beth said. "There's nothing like a linear equation."

We packed up and became Hawthornes again but I missed being the Bighorns; I liked the name printed on placards and tickets, the name that suggested identity was mutable. In the spring, our mother discovered our father had been having an affair with a woman in his office and he had one name for it, *stepping out,* which made it sound as if he'd gone for a walk in a pretty forest, while our mother had another, *betrayal,* which made it sound as if he ought to be beheaded. That trip to the mountains, when I was fourteen, was our last family vacation.

There were names for places I loved and names for animals I'd lost, that would not come home, no matter how I called for them. I was learning to classify things in my science class: kingdom, phylum, class, order, family, genus, species. My mother took back her maiden name when I was in high school; later, when I went away to college, she remarried and changed her last name to Jones.

"David wanted me to," she said, when I asked.

My mother seemed like a different person when I went to visit her in a mansion by the sea where all the photographs were of elegant, tanned people I did not know. She told me her new husband could *see* her, that his love made her feel real.

Beth longed to have her first name legally changed, and she stopped writing it on forms after her ski accident, pretending it didn't exist. But I have been Hazel Hawthorne all my life, and my father was always Henry Hawthorne, except for that week at the ski lodge, before our family scattered.

Christopher Columbus discovered one place, and pretended it was another; I remember the animal that might have been a bear or might have been a Bigfoot, on that last holiday in the Blue Ridge Mountains, watching me from the woods. I remember a stray cat that was fed by everyone on our street: how he responded to at least eight names calling him from porches, shaking bowls of food. Have I mentioned how Mata Hari was shot by a firing squad? How Henry Hudson became a river after he was abandoned by his mutinous crew?

Other Books by Faith Shearin

The Owl Question	May Swenson Award, Utah State University Press, April 2004
The Empty House	Word Poetry, November 2008
Moving the Piano	Stephen F. Austin University Press, November 2011
Telling the Bees	Stephen F. Austin University Press, April 2015
Orpheus, Turning	Dogfish Head Poetry Prize, Broadkill River Press, May 2015
Darwin's Daughter	Stephen F. Austin University Press, April 2018
Lost Language	Press 53, October 2020

It takes courage to grow up
and become who you really are.

e. e. cummings

My Writer's Notebook

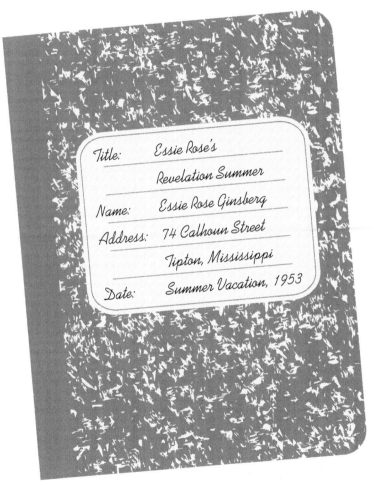

Title: Essie Rose's
          Revelation Summer
Name: Essie Rose Ginsberg
Address: 74 Calhoun Street
          Tipton, Mississippi
Date: Summer Vacation, 1953

To the Reader

Dear Reader,

   This story was mine and mine alone to tell.

   I was an Old Soul child growing up in the deep South in the 1950s, a member of the only Jewish family in a town where there were so many things I did not understand; for instance, the Jim Crow laws that kept people separated by their skin tone. African Americans were called colored people back then, which is why I chose to use that term in this story. They were not allowed to go into certain public places like libraries or sit at lunch counters. I knew of these first hand, because my best and only friend, our African-American house-keeper, Delphia, always had to wait outside for me.

   Even though I was white, not "colored," I, too, felt segregated. I was the odd-girl out. Not only was I of a different faith than the rest of my town, I was shy, and my parents owned a store on the "wrong side of the tracks" where the African-American people did their shopping. But lucky for me I had Delphia to nurture my Old Soul. We were "two peas in a pod," as she used to tell me. It was Delphia's love and devotion to me that became my inspiration for writing this historical fiction novel.

It is my fondest hope that you, my readers, might take your inspiration from Essie Rose Ginsberg's journey, that you muster your own courage and make your voices heard.

Now don't fret, get on with your business and make yourselves proud.

Deanie Yasner

New Hope, Pennsylvania

June 2019

The Letter

Tuesday, June 23

There are so many things I DO NOT UNDERSTAND. Like, for instance, why our end-of-the year school party had to be so hurtful thanks to Donna Sue Hicks. I swear I will never set foot inside Robert E. Lee Elementary School again.

Donna Sue slammed the last crumbly chocolate cupcake on my desk. The whole class turned their heads and stared at me. "Oh," she said smiling, "I almost forgot you."

Then Mary Jo Jamison, Donna Sue's partner in crime, handed me a vanilla ice cream Dixie Cup.

"Me, too, I almost forgot you. Sorry it's half-melted." They looked at each other and giggled.

I was so wishing Miss Williams would point her long wooden ruler toward the door and shout, "Donna Sue Hicks and Mary Jo Jamison, march yourselves down to the principal's office right this minute for those unkind words I heard you say to Essie Rose!"

I was all ready to point my sharpened yellow No.2 pencil at the two of them. "Good riddance! I hope Mr. McCallister makes you both stay there one whole hour after the last bell rings!"

But Miss Williams didn't say a single word.

As usual, neither did I.

Like always, I turned my eyes away and scrunched down in my chair. I grabbed my Social Studies book, the only one big enough to hide my face from 25 pairs of eyes staring straight at me.

Things went from bad to worse when I was walking home and realized the same two mean girls had followed me to the drinking fountain by the main gate of Tipton, Mississippi's one and only Ben Ray Edwards Municipal Swimming Pool.

Donna Sue tucked her long blonde hair behind her

ears. Then she leaned over and splashed water in my face just as I was about to take my first cooling-off mouthful.

"We'll wave to you when we pass the kiddie pool every day, won't we, Mary Jo?"

"Of course we will, Donna Sue," Mary Jo said.

I wiped my face with my tee-shirt and pretended two things. Number one, their teasings didn't make one bit of difference. Number two, I wasn't getting madder at myself by the minute for not being able to tell them what they were doing was plain rotten.

Things went from worse to worst in front of the First Baptist Church. A long plastic banner with purple capital letters was strung from one end of the church to the other.

Donna Sue, who was chosen "Little Miss Tipton" in fourth grade, marched in front of me with her hands hugging her hips and read the sign aloud: "SUMMER BIBLE SCHOOL BEGINS JULY 15. ALL ARE WELCOME!" And in her I'm-So-Sure-of-Myself voice she proclaimed, "Except you, of course, Essie Rose Ginsberg. My mama said your family doesn't believe what we believe so our Bible School is not for the likes of you. This is not where you belong. Right, Mary Jo?"

Mary Jo, who should have been chosen "Little Miss Follow the Leader," piped up in her high-pitched voice, "Right and right!"

My face felt hotter than the Mississippi sun beating down on my head. If I were brave enough to have said what I WANTED to say with those right words Pearlie May says are somewhere deep inside me, I would have told them I didn't need their First Baptist Church Summer Bible School. I had my own Bible School where I DID belong.

In fact I had not one but two. I had my Daddy's Old Testament Friday Night Bible Lessons. Even better, I had my Pearlie May's Every Day Breakfast Bible Lessons. They were really her AHAs! and understandings of what's good and true and right. They came from TWO Bible books, she said – the Old Testament AND the New Testament – and they could sprout up anytime anywhere as long as they came straight from the heart. Knowing all that took a long time coming, which is why Pearlie May said she called it a revelation.

Come to think of it, Summer Bible School or not, Donna Sue and Mary Jo wouldn't understand a word of Pearlie May's lessons. For that matter, they wouldn't

understand anything I'd be doing this summer. Like
for instance, my writing in this Writer's Notebook the
way I've done every summer since Second Grade when
I won the Catherine Lee Whitcome Library Contest.
That's when Miss Beaumont declared me an Honest-
To-Goodness Writer and gave me my very first Writer's
Notebook. Donna Sue and Mary Jo wouldn't care that
I can write anything, about anyone, anytime, any way I
choose. This summer I might even try doing some of
Miss Beaumont's creative writing exercises to help me
with my descriptions.

If only Donna Sue and Mary Jo knew Miss
Beaumont chose ME, Essie Rose Ginsberg, to be
the very first reader of that new book *Charlotte's Web*.
Though I still don't know why because it's about a
spider and a pig and she knows I like my stories true.

They'd never understand why I love to visit Daddy's
variety store on Murdock Row. It's on the wrong side of
the GM&O Railroad tracks where the colored people
of Tipton do their shopping. I didn't know there was
a wrong side until I overheard Donna Sue's mama use
those words. Now what she said got me to thinking. If
Daddy's store was on the right side of the railroad tracks,
would I or wouldn't I get so many teasings?

Come to think of it, I don't understand how being on one side or the other side of a railroad track has anything to do with right or wrong. Anyway, if Donna Sue and Mary Jo ever found out that piece of information, I know I'd be in for even worse teasings than what they dished out today.

I can only imagine what they'd say about my hanging out with Pearlie May, which I would never, ever tell them. What I wanted to say was, "Donna Sue and Mary Jo, you are mean, pig-headed and stupid" If only I'd been brave enough. Of course, if I said those words and Pearlie May learned about it, she'd have my head.

"Get your tall skinny self over here right now!" she'd say. And then I'd be in for a Pearlie May You-Forgot-to-Mind-Your-Mouth scolding.

All I wanted was to get myself home to my best and only friend Pearlie May Gibbs for one of our Two-Peas-in-a-Pod hugs and even a Thinking-On Time about this sorry day.

I ran past the Catherine Lee Whitcome Public Library so fast I knocked down the sign announcing the August 1 Tipton, Mississippi, Centennial Celebration:

One Hundred Years in the Wheel of Progress and I kept on going. I was that angry.

I kept on running with the sweat pouring down my face, past all those big old prim and proper houses on Magnolia Avenue standing tall and important, not like me or my house that we rent.

One more block to go and I'd be safe because that's how Pearlie May makes me feel. And I'd be yanking open our squeaky kitchen screen door. One more block and I'd be yelling, "Pearlie May! Pearlie May! I'm home! School's out. It's time to start planning my Number 11 Birthday." I was certain this would be the birthday Pearlie May thought I'd finally be ready to hear the story of her red bandana. The one she wore every day. The one I stared at with what she called my dark Old Soul eyes she always said looked just like hers.

But none of that ever happened, all because of Pearlie May's note I found waiting for me on the kitchen table. There it was, propped up on her tall cracked coffee cup, the one she used every morning.

Maybe copying Pearlie May's exact words right here will help me understand them. Or maybe not.

Miz Essie Rose,

You know I love you like my own kin and I'd never leave like this if I could help it, but something has happened to my sister Flora Belle over in Spring City. She's taken real sick and has no other kin. I promise to get back soon as I can.

I'll try for Tipton's Fourth of July Picnic, or if not, then for Tipton's August 1 Big Birthday. But no matter what for YOUR August 16th Birthday.

Don't you fret now, child. Get on with your business and make me proud.

Your Pearlie May

No Fretting

Wednesday, June 24

It's almost bedtime. I've wasted the whole day moping and fretting, and I still haven't figured out a single thing. Like, for instance, why Pearlie May up and left.

I remember clear as a bell the day she promised me she'd never leave. It was the day we met. I heard a knock at the kitchen door. Mama said, "Essie Rose, I'll bet it's Pearlie May Gibbs, the woman I hired to look after you and the house. Let's go welcome her."

Pearlie May took one long look into my eyes. Then she took my hand. She held it tight and said, "Why you must be Miz Essie Rose. You're the child I've been waiting for. I know right away we're Two-Peas-in-a-Pod, and I'm going to mind you 'til you don't need minding any more. I'm never going to leave you...no matter what."

But she did.

Now that she's gone and I can't have our Two-Peas-in-a-Pod hug, the only thing I'm left to hug is Sophia, the cloth doll Pearlie May made for me when I was five. That's how old I was when Pearlie May first came to help us, and the first birthday we had together. We had just moved here from up North because Daddy believed he could make a better living for us down South like other Jewish storekeepers he'd heard about. "What I am ever going to do now, Sophia?" I kept asking, hugging her harder than ever while I cried.

I know that was silly. I know cloth dolls can't speak. But for now, talking to Sophia makes me feel like I'm with Pearlie May. For now Sophia is all I have. Come to think of it, Sophia Sunday is the only doll I've ever had and the only one I've ever wanted. I never wanted one of those Toni dolls that Donna Sue talked about at school, bragging to all the other girls how she spent hours giving her Toni doll a permanent. No, Sophia Sunday is the one and only doll for me.

Holding Sophia, fingering her black yarn hair, makes me remember how Pearlie May and I named her.

"Her name's Sophia," I told Pearlie May, "because Sophia sounds strong and sure and that's how I want to be someday." It was Pearlie May who insisted she have a last name. A whole name.

"Then you pick," I said. Pearlie May didn't blink an eye.

"Sunday, that's what her second name must be for sure, child, because I've spent more than a month of my praise days making her. That's all there is to it."

Another thing I still can't believe: our Thinking-On Time didn't happen yesterday, the one I needed so I could tell Pearlie May about the mean teasings that had happened at school and on my way home. I know she'd tell me not to worry my 10-going-on-20-year-old-head about anything Donna Sue and Mary Jo said or did. She'd say, "Child, they don't know any better. Just because all your right words are stuck deep inside you doesn't mean that's the way it's always going to be. The day will come when they'll bubble up and you'll say what you need to say the way I taught you to say it. I'm sure of it."

Well, I'm not so sure of it.

Having my own Thinking-On Time with Sophia Sunday here in bed got me fretting about Pearlie May's note: *Get on with your business and make me proud!*

What IS my business I'm supposed to get on with? As far as I'm concerned, my business is noticing, worrying, reading, and, of course, my number one best thing I do: writing.

Other than that, I don't do much else. I do take pictures with the Brownie camera I redeemed for Mama's twelve books of S&H Green stamps from Kroger. The pictures are tucked away in that old red-and-black checkered hat box Mama brought from up North. And that's where they're staying – right next to the dried four-leaf clover Pearlie May and I found last summer and my filled-in Writer's Notebooks.

But I don't think picture taking is what Pearlie May meant.

So I'm trying to stop my worrying and fretting. After all, Pearlie May did say she'd try her best to be home for the Fourth of July and that's only days away and Pearlie May always does what she says.

Just now I crayoned "NO FRETTING" in purple on a blank piece of paper and Scotch-taped it to the back of my door, right above my sign that reads "DON'T TWIRL YOUR HAIR!" (as a just-in-case reminder).

I'm back in bed with the sheet pulled over me, using my flashlight so I can see to write. It's way too hot for me to snuggle under my favorite purple-striped quilt. I'm too tired to write another word. Except...

I, ESSIE ROSE GINSBERG, PROMISE TO FIGURE OUT MY BUSINESS

AND I PROMISE TO MAKE PEARLIE MAY PROUD.

Thunder and Trouble

Thursday, June 25

It's been a long day. I'm tired from writing too late last night. I had planned to sleep until lunchtime today, but loud booms of thunder roaring across the sky and bright streaks of lightning coming through my curtains woke me up at the crack of dawn.

If Pearlie May were here she'd be sitting on my bed saying, "Child, no need to be scared. The thunder, why that's the Good Lord rolling his potatoes around. And the rain, why that's going to make my daisies grow. And all that lightning, why that's the Good Lord's artwork."

She always finished with, "You're safe and sound.

I'm right here." And I always finished with, "That's where I want you to be until I'm umpteen years old."

Anyway, I didn't want to fret, so I decided to pull my shade down, cover my ears and go back to sleep.

I finally woke up when I heard Mama call New York City and her only sister.

"Good morning, Rachael, I need to talk to you," I heard her say.

I'm guessing she didn't want Daddy to hear her conversation. That's probably why she came home from the store. One thing I've noticed ever since I realized I was a noticer: Mama will go to any lengths to keep Daddy from getting riled up. They both will go to any lengths to keep what they consider "grown-up" matters a secret from me.

I shouldn't have, but I listened in on the phone conversation. This is what I heard, but wish I hadn't.

Mama told Aunt Rachael that she is worried about Daddy lately. She said that Daddy gets upset over every little thing, not just his usual upset. Like, for instance, if she makes something other than meat and potatoes for dinner. She thought maybe it had something to do with Daddy's saying things like this slow sleepy town isn't anything like New York. That's why he's missing the hustle and bustle, the skyscrapers and especially his childhood synagogue.

Then Mama told Aunt Rachael she wondered if Daddy's nerves got jangled by that New York newspaper article she'd sent about mischief makers down South marking up stores owned by Jewish merchants with troubling words like "JEW STORE."

"Things are beginning to change here," Mama said in a voice I never heard her use before. It was all quivery.

So now I think I may have a new worry and one I can't do anything about. I'm wondering what "things are changing" means. All I know is, it better not mean we'll have to leave. We can't budge from this house until Pearlie May comes back.

Two Important Things

Friday, June 26

Wow. Two important things happened to me this morning.

Important Thing Number One: I am officially the very first reader of the library's copy of *Charlotte's Web*.

When I left the house to go check it out, I didn't pay one iota of attention to Mattie Lou Davis, the woman Mama hired as "a substitute housekeeper just until Pearlie May gets back." As far as I'm concerned, she has three strikes against her.

1. She doesn't act like Pearlie May.

2. She doesn't cook like Pearlie May.

3. She's not Pearlie May Gibbs in any size, shape or form.

Mama says she's fine, just a "substitute," but I say there is no "substitute" for Pearlie May. THAT'S ALL THERE IS TO THAT.

So I waltzed right past Mattie Lou Davis and out the kitchen door and headed straight to the Catherine Lee Whitcome Public Library, my favorite building in all of Tipton, Mississippi. The morning was already hot and steamy, so I stopped for a break at the very step Pearlie May used to sit on when we went to the library together. I'd ask her to go inside with me every single time, until one day she said, "Miz Essie Rose, don't you ask me that anymore. I do declare, child, you know colored folks aren't welcome inside. Now fix those red glasses high on your nose and run on and get your books. I'll be resting on this very step until you come out."

Sometimes she'd add, "A rest will do me good. You know I'm no spring chicken anymore." Mostly I pretended I didn't hear those last few words. Things like that could get me twirling my hair in no time flat.

Come to think of it, Pearlie May not being welcome inside the library is another one of those things I DO NOT UNDERSTAND.

Since I love to read so much, I'm happy Miss Catherine Lee Whitcome, who founded the library in 1915 so everyone could have a book, decided to do that because Mama and Daddy say they can't afford to buy me every book I want to read. "Not with business falling off at the store," Daddy says. He repeats those same words often.

The minute I walked through the door, Miss Beaumont cornered me, though I don't know how she was able to see me past the face-high stack of flyers she was holding.

"Essie Rose Ginsberg," she said, "I'll bet you came to pick up the copy of *Charlotte's Web* I saved for you." Miss Beaumont disappeared, then I heard a loud thump when she dumped the stack of flyers on her desk.

"Wait two seconds," she said, slightly out of breath. "Here's your book and here's a flyer. Essie Rose Ginsberg, you must read every word on this Centennial flyer before you leave this library." She had that look in her eyes and that tone in her voice that warned me I'd better listen and do what she said.

So I went outside and sat myself down on Pearlie May's step and read the first few lines.

TIPTON, MISSISSIPPI CENTENNIAL 1853-1953
ONE HUNDRED YEARS IN THE WHEEL OF
PROGRESS

ATTENTION CHILDREN!

Announcing Tipton's Centennial Children's Writing Contest
Theme: Celebrating Tipton's Five Best Heroes

I was about to read the details when I noticed Donna Sue and Mary Jo walking past the library.

Important Thing Number Two: I could tell from Donna Sue's ruffled swimsuit cover-up and Mary Jo's striped beach towel, they were on their way to the swimming pool. I pretended I didn't see them, but my pretending didn't work. Before I could figure out my next move, they marched up to me, one on either side. I knew I was in for another mean teasing.

"Essie Rose, why don't you come to the pool with us?" Donna Sue asked. Then she winked at Mary Jo.

"Yeah, Essie Rose, why don't you come to the pool with us?" Mary Jo asked.

I wish I hadn't stopped on Pearlie May's step to read that flyer.

I wish Pearlie May would have been on her step waiting for me.

I wish I could have blurted out some comeback words, like, for instance, "MIND YOUR MOUTHS."

But they were only wishes.

I'm happy to say they decided to go about their business before they had a chance to notice the tears running down my cheeks.

I will never try to get along with Donna Sue and Mary Jo no matter what Pearlie May tried to drum into my head about needing to be extra nice to folks who haven't learned the first thing about how to get along with other folks. She'd say, "Child, no person is all bad. We all have some good points, even those girls who haven't learned to show them yet."

Well, how long am I supposed to wait for either Donna Sue or Mary Jo to show me one good point? Right now it feels like forever.

Anyway, by this time I was too rattled to read about the writing contest or think about who I'd even choose as my hero. So I tossed the flyer into my backpack along with *Charlotte's Web* and walked home.

Only one thing happened to me this afternoon, but it was very important.

It all started when I noticed I am using up pencils really fast and thinking this might turn into my busiest writing summer ever. But I don't mind because this way I'm guaranteed not to forget anything important like, for instance, all the ways I'm trying to get on with my business and make Pearlie May proud. I'll have everything I want to share with her written down, waiting for her.

I needed more pencils to refill the burlap pencil bag that Pearlie May made for me. I remember the exact day she gave it to me. She declared, "Lordie, Miz Essie Rose, sometimes you are a bit messy. I'm mighty tired of picking up your pencils scattered all over this floor every day. Besides, I'm getting too old to take a fall."

I gave her a big thank you and my best Two-Peas-in-a-Pod hug.

"Pearlie May," I said as I stared at her wire-rimmed glasses crooked like always and low on her nose. "You will never find another Essie Rose Ginsberg pencil on this floor ever again."

Anyway, I headed to Daddy's store for more No. 2

pencils. I walked down Commerce Street past my two favorite stores – Woolworth's Five and Dime where I usually stop for some window shopping, and Latham's Rexall Drugstore where I usually stop for a vanilla ice cream float or a cherry Coke. But today I skipped both. Instead, I turned left on Main Street, walked to the end and crossed over the tracks to Murdock Row.

Daddy's variety store is the sixth one on the block, between Andy's Shoe Shop on one side and Lenora's Luncheonette on the other. For some reason, I always hum Pearlie May's humming song when I walk down Murdock Row. Maybe it's to keep me from fretting about those wrong side of the tracks words Donna Sue's mother said. Those words could start my Old Soul turning topsy-turvy in no time flat. Like, for instance, making me wonder if I belong on either side of the tracks in this town with rules I don't understand and never will.

Daddy always talks about how he prides himself in carrying everything from soup to nuts in his store. Only then he jokes (and that doesn't happen often) that he doesn't actually carry either one, just everything else in between. "Everything all my customers need is right here," and then he adds, "at affordable prices."

My favorite aisles (in order) are:

Aisle Number One: paper, pens, and pencils

Aisle Number Five: candy and Crackerjacks

Aisle Number Eight: ribbons and rick-rack

I know trouble when I see it, and I knew there was trouble the minute I noticed the front door propped wide open. Daddy had his sleeves rolled up and his hands were wrist-deep in a tin bucket filled with soapy water.

Mama was yelling from the back of the store, "Max, are you finished yet? Do you need more soap and water?"

Daddy yelled back, "No thank you, Tillie. I'm finished. I've rubbed off the words."

"What words?" I asked him, though I don't know why I even bothered. I should have known what his answer would be.

"None that concern you, Essie Rose. It's all taken care of," Daddy said. "You go and get whatever you need. I've got to help Bernice now with her layaway."

I wanted to know what the words were. At least I thought I did, but I knew enough to heed Daddy's warning. I picked up my pencils and my two Milky Way bars. One for now and one to freeze for later.

I usually hang out at the store for a while, but today did not feel like the right time for that.

"Bye and thanks," I said. Daddy barely nodded. Mama called my name from the back of the store.

"Essie, dear, with all the commotion, I almost forgot. Tonight we greet the Shabbos. Remember to ready the table." Like I'd ever forget.

All the way home I spent time thinking on grown-up matters. Like, for instance, I wondered about the looks on Mama and Daddy's faces. I wondered what those words were that Daddy rubbed off the front door. They could have been those words I heard Mama say to Aunt Rachael – JEW STORE – but those words were way too scary for me to keep locked inside my head. So I erased them lickety-split. I hummed Pearlie May's favorite song, "Swing Low, Sweet Chariot" three times walking home.

I also thought about Mama and Daddy always working in the store from morning to night. I wonder if that's the reason I don't get many hugs. They don't have much time for anything else, including me. But Pearlie May does.

I wondered about other things, too. I wondered about all the many words I wish I'd said to Donna Sue and Mary Jo but didn't.

"Pearlie May," I yelled the minute I opened the kitchen door, "I need a Thinking-On Time." Then I remembered Pearlie May was gone.

I guess our Thinking-On Time has to wait. But I hope not for long. I checked the calendar and counted the squares. July fourth is just eight days away.

The Plan, Part 1

Saturday, June 27

I've heard Mama and Daddy say over and over how they wished they could close the store on Shabbos, our Holy Day. But Daddy says, "Saturday's 9-to-9 business day practically pays the monthly rent." Daddy also says renting is more prudent.

Up until Pearlie May left, Saturday got to be our Two-Peas-in-a-Pod special day. Besides always going to the movies, she would plan a surprise. Like, for instance, taking me pond fishing or flower picking. Sometimes, she'd even take me to her house. I'd get to stay until

Mama and Daddy picked me up late at night. That was always my favorite surprise.

So now I had to figure out just how I would spend this longest day of the week without Pearlie May by my side.

I nixed Mama's advice to go swimming. Donna Sue and Mary Jo are always at the pool, from the time it opens until it closes. And after their hateful teasing and that miserable experience last summer when they stared at me because I held on to the side of the pool for two hours, I decided I'd never go back no matter how many times they tried to trick me into it. I never want to hear Donna Sue yell, "Watch me do a backflip off the high dive" again. Better still, I never want to listen to Mary Jo's namby-pamby echoes, "I'm watching, I'm watching." Come to think on it, I wonder if Mary Jo has ever had one real thought of her own. If she did, I'd sure like to be the first one to know what it was.

No, the pool was definitely not for me, even though the thermometer outside the kitchen window said it was 95 degrees already and a dip in the cool water would really perk me up.

Of course, I did have that new library book, and now I know why Miss Beaumont wanted me to read

Charlotte's Web. It's very exciting. Once I started it, I couldn't wait to find out what happened to Wilbur, the runt-of-the-litter piglet that Fern saved before her father could swing his axe and kill him.

I cried a little when Wilbur was sent to Uncle Lurvy's farm. But at least Fern can visit him. I can't visit Pearlie May now. I read on to the chapter where Wilbur the pig met Charlotte the Spider, who, just like Pearlie May, knew more than a thing or two about friendship.

Like, for instance, Charlotte knew how to calm Wilbur, and Pearlie May knows how to calm me.

Another thing that made Charlotte special was her way with words. I swear she is an Honest-to-Goodness-Writer, too. In fact, I'm making a separate page in this notebook for a Charlotte, The Spider Word List. SALUTATIONS is the first word on the list.

As much as I wanted to keep on reading, I decided to take a break and as Miss Beaumont says, "Let the characters settle inside me."

So I finally decided on my third Saturday choice, even though I knew it would cause me to fret. I'd go to the movies. But this time it would be without Pearlie May.

That got me thinking about what she'd told me

at least a hundred times. She'd say, "Sometimes, child, you got to do what you got to do, even if it's not easy. I call it shoring up your courage to do what's right or else you'll never be your best self."

I remember asking her, "Pearlie May, how is it you always know exactly what to say?"

"Child," she'd say, "I suppose it comes from studying about life, the hard way, the same as my mama did."

"How many of these right word sayings do you have?" I asked.

"Only six. I call them my Half Dozen Words of Wisdom. That's all a person needs. And I love you so much I have to tell them to you over and over until I know for sure you have them in your pretty little 10-going-on-20-year-old stubborn pig-tailed head."

Then she'd laugh so hard her red bandana wiggled. "That is until you get one of your 10-year-old hissy fits."

(Oh, I did it again. I digressed, as Miss Beaumont calls it. But she says that's what writers do, and it can make their writing more interesting. I hope she's right.)

Well, I shored up my courage. I took myself to the Ritz Theatre to watch a Saturday afternoon Roy Rogers Double Feature Western – *Sunset in the West* and *Pals of the Golden West*, to be exact. Today when I sat downstairs, I looked up toward the balcony where Pearlie May would have been sitting. I closed my eyes hard and wished she were there.

I had a big surprise later today. I was walking down Magnolia Avenue past the big and important homes where the big and important people in town live. Mama calls them "antebellum Southern mansions" because they remind her of the movie *Gone with the Wind*. When I neared the Buford's big important home, I heard the sounds of a harmonica – loud and clear.

I was certain that's what it was because Daddy sells them in his store and I tried playing one a time or two. Well. I stopped dead in my tracks.

Whoever was playing that harmonica was playing Pearlie May's humming tune, "Swing Low, Sweet Chariot," the tune I missed hearing every day.

I had to investigate, but how? I'm just Essie Rose Ginsberg who doesn't really belong on this street.

That's when I figured out My Plan. I'd pretend to be somebody else. And that somebody else would be, of course, daring detective Nancy Drew, like in her mystery book *The Clue of the Tapping Heels*, the only one

I've ever read because our fourth-grade teacher said it was mandatory. But now I'm glad Miss Simmons made us read it because I could use some of Nancy's ideas for my own sleuthing. And I did.

I snuck inside the Buford's metal gate – close enough to where I caught a glimpse of a boy sitting on the front porch swing playing a harmonica. MYSTERY SOLVED. Like a good sleuth, I took out my notebook and wrote down a description of him. I noticed he was brown skinned and wore overalls with brass buckled straps, a white tee-shirt, high-topped sneakers tied all the way to the top, and a baseball cap turned backwards. He could maybe be in third grade. Or fourth?

I stood still as a statue. With my eyes closed, I listened to him play Pearlie May's tune three more times. When he stopped playing, I opened my eyes and watched as he put the harmonica in his pocket and picked up a big pad of paper.

I squinted, but all I could see was his hand moving up and down the page. Now, to come up with the next part of My Plan so I can actually meet that boy on the porch swing.

Meeting new people, colored or white, is not what I do best. Every kid in my class knows I'm shy. Come to think of it, maybe that's another reason I don't have any friends my age. Of course, being the only Jewish student at Robert E. Lee Elementary School, or for that matter, in Tipton, doesn't help any either.

Besides, I know the rules here in Tipton, Mississippi. Colored kids don't talk to white kids and white kids don't talk to colored kids.

Another thing I DO NOT UNDERSTAND.

Sunday Mind Picture

Sunday, June 28

Sunday is Dress-Up-Go-To-Church Day in Tipton, Mississippi. Except, not for the Ginsbergs. For us, Sunday is Dress-Down-Stay-at-Home Day.

Mama puts on her Sunday apron, the one she inherited from her mama. She makes a special breakfast – Pillsbury Oven Ready Biscuits and sunny-side up eggs. Two eggs for Daddy, one egg for her, and one egg for me. I dip my biscuits in the runny egg yolk. Mama and Daddy dip their biscuits in honey.

The minute we sit down at the table, Daddy always announces, "Tillie and Essie Rose, after having to talk so much in the store, I'd appreciate a quiet meal."

Then Mama always says, "That's a fine idea, Max." I'm not sure if she means it, but from all my noticing I'm sure she does whatever keeps Daddy's nerves from becoming jangled.

I say, "It's fine with me, too," although in secret I wish we could play one of those games we play during snack time at school, like, for instance, Name a Word. It's when one person calls a letter of the alphabet and every other person has to name a word that begins with that letter. If we played it at breakfast, I'd call an *E* for Essie or a *P* for Pearlie May.

After breakfast, we traipse into the living room for our Sunday morning reading of *The Commercial Appeal*. Daddy sits in his old beat-up easy chair and reads the news section. Mama sits on our grey sofa and reads the magazine section. I sprawl out on the rug and read the comics in this order:

"Little Orphan Annie," my first favorite

"Nancy and Sluggo" and "Blondie and Dagwood," my second favorites.

I can't quite figure how she does it, but somehow Mama knows exactly when to put down the magazine section and announce, "It's time for our Sunday ride." That's another thing Daddy likes to do "to get his mind off the store."

We pile in our two-toned brown DeSoto. "It's time to make a Mind Picture," I say to myself the minute we pass the sign on Highway 45 South that reads "Leaving Tipton, Mississippi, Founded in 1853." Besides I've seen enough of all the cotton fields that we've driven by hundreds of times before.

A Mind Picture is something Miss Beaumont taught us writers to write. She described it as a picture, only painted in words. Here is the one I painted in my mind today and am writing now in my Writer's Notebook because I always want to remember it:

> *I'm at Pearlie May's house. I open the screen door and walk inside. Her house is small and plain and neat and clean. I walk into her kitchen and count ten glass Mason jars filled with canned green beans, three pots, and one frying pan — the one she uses to make her secret recipe of Pearlie May's Fabulous Fried Chicken. I see her*

standing at the stove. She keeps her eyes on the pan so she can notice when each piece is golden brown. When all the pieces are ready, we go out on her front porch and eat fried chicken until we're too stuffed to move. After a while, I finally get up, go over and give her a big hug — one I wish could last forever.

The Plan, Part 2

Monday, June 29

Wow. Today was exciting. I came up with Part Two of My Plan to meet that boy on the swing at the Buford's proper house. It worked. I now know his name is Moses Brownridge.

Here's how I did it.

First, I noticed a box of unopened Kroger-bought cookies on the kitchen table when I sat down for breakfast. It had a note Scotch-taped on the top that read "For Mr. and Mrs. Buford."

Mama always makes sure the Bufords have cookies.

When I asked her once how come, she said, "Essie, you know Daddy and I believe in doing Mitzvahs." Then she always adds, "Like Daddy says, doing good deeds is what our Jewish religion is all about. We being the only Jews in town, we have to set the very best example we can." Mr. Buford, who Mama said used to be the long time President of the First National Bank of Tipton, helped Daddy when we moved here and Mama knows he and his wife can't get out so easy now.

Usually I choose not to think too much about Daddy's rules. They make me feel different. And I'm different enough already – with my red glasses and my Old Soul ways and having zero friends other than, of course, Pearlie May. But this time, Daddy's Mitzvah rule fit right into My Plan.

Since Mama had already left for the store, I declared myself to be the Deliverer-of-the-Cookies. I decided they had to look especially pretty today. So I opened the box and arranged the cookies in a circle on one of Mama's glass platters, covered them with plastic wrap and waltzed off to the Buford's without any explaining to Mattie Lou Davis.

And that's how I met Moses. With my very own

eyes, I saw him sitting on the front porch swing. With my very own ears, I heard him playing Pearlie May's tune on his harmonica.

"Hi," I said. "I'm Essie Rose Ginsberg. What's your name?" (That alone took some mustering up of my courage.) At first he didn't answer. Then he looked up at me and said, "I'm Moses Brownridge and I'm supposed to be sitting on this swing practicing my harmonica for our church summer celebration and getting on with my business. That's what my Mama told me."

I must have gasped because I saw Moses' eyes get big. But I couldn't believe his words. "That's exactly what my friend Pearlie May told ME to do!"

From then on, I chatterbox talked and Moses did the listening. When he did say something, out came words I had gotten used to hearing in Tipton, Mississippi, but still didn't understand. Like, for instance, he said, "Mama told me it wasn't a good idea for a colored boy to be talking to a white girl." So I quit my chatterboxing except to ask Moses if he'd find a way to make sure Mr. and Mrs. Buford got their Ginsberg Mitzvah cookies.

I handed Moses the platter. "Thank you," I said as I turned back toward the metal gate. I didn't want to say another word because, for sure, I didn't want to make trouble for Moses.

On the way home, I wondered if doing a good deed and being kind to a stranger could be the same thing as getting on with my business? Would this make Pearlie May proud?

Right now, though, I'm wondering about something different – what I heard Daddy say when Mama and Daddy came home from the store last night.

Here's what he said: "I heard those storekeepers myself, Tillie. Mr. Thompson from the hardware store and Mr. Benson from the clothing store and Mr. Douglas, our Deputy Mayor, and yes, even Mr. Chesterfield from the *Tipton Daily Gazette* joined in as well. They said colored people in this town are getting too uppity."

Even though I wasn't exactly sure what "uppity" meant, it didn't sound good. I needed to warn Pearlie May. I wrote a note in big letters and Scotch-taped it to the back of my bedroom door.

BE SURE TO TELL PEARLIE MAY WHEN SHE COMES BACK TO BE CAREFUL.

A Wish

Tuesday, June 30

This is my Fourth of July wish. I hope I won't jinx it by writing it down.

I wish that Pearlie May will be home in time for me to watch her make her fabulous fried chicken, sample her warm apple pie, help her pack and unpack Mama's picnic basket, and play "Guess What I See?" with her in the back seat of the car while Mama and Daddy listen to President Dwight David Eisenhower's speech on the radio. And maybe for the first time ever, she can stay and eat with us on our side of the James S. Wilkins

Memorial State Park because to me, she's family like my up-North family – Aunt Rachael, Uncle David, and my cousins Sammy and Julie.

The Worry Jar

Wednesday, July 1

It's officially July according to the Kroger "Flowers of Mississippi" calendar on my desk. But Pearlie May has not come home.

I've spent the day twirling my pig-tails, but not into the knots I do when I get really worried – knots that took Pearlie May two hours to untangle one day. That's when she decided to take matters into her own hands. That very day she surprised me with a Worry Jar made from one of her emptied-out Mason jars.

"Miz Essie Rose," she said, "I'm not about to spend all day combing tangles out of your pretty little pig-tailed head. From now on, child, when you feel a troublesome worry and I'm talking about a real troublesome one coming on, you grab one of your pencils, write down your worry, drop it inside this Worry Jar I made for you and let that be that. No more two-hour tangles to undo."

Then she looked me in the eye. "Remember child," she said, "all worries are not equal. You need to think on that."

Well, I thought on it, and decided that Pearlie May not being home does not qualify as a bona fide Worry Jar Worry because Pearlie May DID say she'd do her best to make it back in time for the Fourth of July Picnic. Pearlie May always does what she says she'll do.

With that worry out of the way, I curled up in bed with Sophia Sunday to read more about Charlotte and Wilbur. But then I managed to get distracted by that flyer Miss Beaumont handed me the other day. I figured it might be a good idea to take another look. After all, I am an Honest-To-Goodness Writer. I do like the theme of Celebrating Tipton's Five Best Heroes. I also know something about heroes from Mr. Wilder's history class, and even more from listening to Daddy's Friday Night Bible Lessons, the ones he tells me over and over because he says they represent the best people in the Old Testament Bible.

I couldn't think right away who I'd choose for a present-day Tipton Best Hero, but I read through all the rules in case I figured out someone. I'm in the right age range. And I know I can write 300 words because I wrote that many and even more when I was in third grade.

I began to wonder how it might feel to see my winning entry in the special edition of the *Tipton Daily Gazette*. But since I didn't have the slightest clue who I'd write about, I put down the flyer and picked up my book to read more about Charlotte and Wilbur like I had intended to do in the first place. I broke my One-Chapter-at-a-Time Rule because when Charlotte began devising her word plan to keep Wilbur alive, I could not stop turning the pages.

I'm glad I took a quick break to add two new words to my special Charlotte the Spider Word List – TERRIFIC and RADIANT.

It was right then that I heard three knocks on the kitchen door. "Just a minute," I yelled out. "I'm on my way."

Wow was I ever surprised when I laid my eyes on none other than Moses Brownridge. And while he wouldn't come in, we had the best conversation sitting on my favorite steps.

"Essie," he started off, "Mama sent me over to return your platter, but she told me to be quick. Just get on with my business and get on home."

"Well," I said, putting my hands on my hips, "that makes two of us. I'm getting on with my business trying to make Pearlie May proud like she asked me to do when she up and left."

"Left for where?" Moses asked.

"Over to Spring City to take care of her sick sister Flora Belle. She's trying to make it back for the Fourth of July picnic. I can't imagine a Fourth of July picnic without her. She's my best and only friend. It's been that way for five, almost six years. I really miss her."

Moses looked away. He cleared his throat. "I know a heap about missing. My pa. He's been gone a while. He went up North looking for some steady work."

I got quiet. So did Moses. But then all of a sudden, HE became Mr. Chatterbox. Like, for instance, telling me how he found ways to help with his missing, how he learned to play the harmonica his pa gave him before he left, and how he drew his pa's picture so he'd always remember what he looked like.

"I keep it with me all the time," he said. "I look at it whenever I get lonesome." Then Moses asked me a question I didn't expect.

"What does your friend look like?" I closed my eyes and told him.

"My friend is tall. She has dark Old Soul eyes she says are like mine. She has a big smile that shows all the wrinkles on her face. And she wears a red bandana tied around her head." I was tempted to tell Moses about the promise Pearlie May made to tell me the story when she thought I was ready to hear it, but decided I didn't know Moses well enough for that.

"Oh," I chatterboxed on, "she wears round glasses, too. Like mine."

Finally, I stopped talking to ask Moses a question of my own. "Is your pa coming back any time soon?"

Moses tapped his foot. He looked down.

"Don't know," he whispered. Then he looked up and said, "Do know I'd better get on home before my mama threatens me with a switch from one of those big old oak trees in the front yard."

Moses ran down Calhoun Street and I ran inside the house. I crossed my fingers on both hands hoping his pa would come home in three days like my Pearlie May.

10

Another Mind Picture

Thursday, July 2

I wrote way too much yesterday, so today I'm going to imagine another Miss Beaumont Mind Picture.

This Mind Picture is of the surprise I know Pearlie May Gibbs will have in store for me when it's July Fourth – unless she gets herself home today or tomorrow.

I'm using my very best cursive writing.

She'll be at the picnic waiting for me. I'll scream, "Pearlie May! Pearlie May! You're back!"

I'll run up and give her a huge whopping hug. And I won't take my eyes off her red bandana, not even as she walks over to the colored people's side. Then I'll wait until she comes back to the white people's side to help pack up. I'll give her another whopping hug and hold her hand all the way to the car. And we'll be together side by side in the back seat like it's supposed to be.

I can't wait!

A Broken Ritual

Friday, July 3

It was SUPPOSED to be our usual Friday night Sabbath dinner, followed by Daddy's Friday Night Bible Lesson.

Daddy says rituals are rituals. Except our rituals are different.

Jewish people usually go to synagogue every Sabbath. But since we're the only Jewish family in town, there is no synagogue in Tipton. The nearest one is two hours away. That's why we only make the trip twice a year. We go for Rosh Hashanah, the day Daddy says is about making peace and striving to be a better person, and Yom Kippur, the day Daddy says is about forgiving and being forgiven. My favorite parts of our Far-Away Holidays are eating apples dipped in honey and staying overnight in a hotel.

Another ritual that is different is what we do for Challah bread. Since we live where there aren't any other Jews, Mama can't just buy it at the bakery. And it's not easy for her to make it since she spends all her time in the store. So Daddy said we had to make another "adaptation." Rabbi Levine from our Far-Away Holiday Synagogue told him we could use store bought rolls or loaves of "un" Challah as long as they were whole and there were two. Daddy didn't go into much detail about the two-loaf thing, though he mentioned something Rabbi Levine told him about the Jews in the desert receiving a double portion of "bread from heaven" on Friday in honor of the Sabbath.

I'm guessing Daddy will explain it better someday – maybe make it one of his Friday Night Bible Stories when I'm older and have more patience to listen. Maybe he knows I like his Hero stories best.

Tonight's ritual was the same as always.

I made sure the table was set way before Mama and Daddy came home from the store. I always do it the same exact way. First, I spread Bubbe's stained embroidered tablecloth over our green Formica table. Mama says no wrinkles.

Next, I carefully set three places with her blue flowered china and matching napkins next to each plate.

Then Mama does her rituals. Like, for instance, she places her old pair of silver candlesticks exactly in the middle of the table. She fills them with tall white candles and reminds me every Friday night they once belonged to Daddy's Mama Rosa. Esther Rosa. Essie Rose.

Then Mama places Daddy's written prayers on top of his place. I don't know why, because he has them memorized.

Like always, Daddy says, "Tillie, make sure the sun is setting."

Like always, Mama looks out the kitchen window. "We can begin."

Mama lights the candles, covers her eyes and recites the blessing.

She says her Daughter Prayer and kisses my head.

Daddy chants the blessings over the wine. We use Welch's Grape Juice, another one of those adaptations. Every Friday night, Daddy says, "Tillie, I do miss the fact that we can't buy wine here in Tipton like we could up North in New York."

Every Friday night, Mama says, "Max, maybe the law will change someday."

I say it doesn't matter to me. Come to think of it, I like Welch's Grape Juice.

Sometimes we all read a psalm together. Mama likes these times best.

Tonight, though, I noticed something different. The rituals were the same, only the order was different. Daddy told his Friday Night Bible Story *before* dinner. He began the lesson the way he always did. He looked into my eyes and said, "Remember, Essie Rose Ginsberg, we're here to try to make the world a better place in whatever way we can."

I had tonight's story memorized, the one about Moses and how he led his people out of Egypt to escape the mean Pharaoh and how after many hard times and struggles he finally delivered God's Ten Commandments to his people. That started me thinking about Pearlie May's Half Dozen Words of Wisdom like, for instance, the one about shoring up your courage. I bet she got that piece of wisdom straight from Moses himself.

After Daddy finished his storytelling, Mama said,

"Let's eat." But I noticed they barely nibbled on the brisket or the roast potatoes or green beans, let alone the lemon Jello with bananas on top.

Finally, Mama put her fork down.

"Essie, honey," she said in her quivery voice, "we received a call at the store today. It was from Pearlie May."

I sat up in my chair. I had a feeling I didn't want to hear another word Mama was about to say.

"It's not going so well for her and her sister Flora Belle," she said. "Pearlie May can't make it back in time for the Fourth of July. She said to tell you how sorry she is."

Mama reached for my hand, but I pulled it away.

"She's MY friend!" I shouted. "Why didn't she call ME?"

I ran off to my room, grabbed Sophia Sunday, and had an honest-to-goodness hissy fit. The kind I had when I got angry, the kind that made Pearlie May shake her head and scold.

"How could you, Pearlie May?" I yelled. "You're supposed to be my friend!"

"We were two Old Souls!" I shouted, "and now there's only one of us here!"

The Picnic

Saturday, July 4

Before the Picnic

My wind-up clock read exactly 2:30 a.m. when I sat down at my desk to write Pearlie May a Knew-I'd-Never-Mail-It letter because Pearlie May knew what I was thinking at 2:30 in the morning or any time, for that matter. But after last night's bad news, I had to write it. I was that angry and that sad.

Here's what it said:

Dear Pearlie May,

I'm so sorry you won't be home for the picnic. I can't believe how terrible it's going to be without you. Now I'll have to watch Donna Sue show off her Double-Dutch jump rope routine. I'll have to listen to Mary Jo scream, "Look over here, Essie Rose!" when they run in the three-legged race with all their friends like they did last year. And now I'll have to do all these things...by myself. You know you are my best and only friend. Please come home soon. I MISS YOU.

Your Essie Rose

P.S. I'm trying to make you proud. I remembered to water your daisies in the front yard. I'm trying to get on with my business, but first I need to figure out what that is. Whatever it is, I'll be doing it without you.

I could feel it coming: a full-blown worry attack. Because come to think of it, if Pearlie May didn't do what she said she'd do this time, she might not do what she said a second time.

My Worry Jar was still empty, but not for long. I wrote on a blank piece of paper in big red letters:

TROUBLESOME WORRY NUMBER ONE
PEARLIE MAY WON'T MAKE IT HOME FOR
THE CENTENNIAL

I dropped my worry in. This better work.

But even if it did work, I realized I had another worry right behind it: how to tell Daddy I absolutely did not want to go to the Picnic. I tossed and turned until the clock read 8:00 a.m., when I was still trying to find my best words, ones that wouldn't get Daddy all riled up.

Except then I realized I couldn't do any better than Templeton the rat in *Charlotte's Web* when he told Wilbur he didn't want to go to his county fair.

I would tell Daddy, "I haven't the fainted interest in fairs." Then I'd say, in my own words, "I'm staying home with Mattie Lou Davis if I have to."

And that's just what I did, even though I knew before the first word came out of my mouth what he'd say.

"Essie Rose," he said, "you will attend. You know it's important for our family to fit in and participate in the town's festivities and it's important to be generous with our time."

Well, I didn't care one iota about fitting in with Tipton's festivities or, for that matter, fitting in with Donna Sue and Mary Jo or anyone else.

The Picnic

At least I was smart enough to bring my camera and notebook. Of course, they couldn't take Pearlie May's place.

The James S. Wilkins Memorial State Park off Highway 45 never changes. The wooden picnic tables were lined up in rows like they were last year – white people's tables on one side and colored people's tables on the other side. We had all the shade trees on our side.

Daddy chose the same table he always does. What we did didn't change this year, only the how of it. Like, for instance, Pearlie May didn't unpack the basket, Mama did. Pearlie May didn't set the table, Mama did.

"Let's eat," she said, after all the food had been placed on the red-and-white checkered plastic tablecloth. But I wasn't the least bit hungry. I nibbled at Mattie Lou Davis' UN-fabulous fried chicken and sipped my Orange Crush until Daddy announced it was time for them to attend to their "community fitting-in job," running the Cake-Walk Booth. No fun for me.

As soon as they left, I grabbed my camera and went looking for a perfect place to take a perfect picture. Like, for instance, one good enough to put into my old red-and-black checkered hat box, to show Pearlie May I was thinking about her and wishing she were here.

It only took a short walk to the tiny wooden bridge that crosses over Little Creek to the colored people's side for me to know I'd found THE place, for sure. I'd take a picture of the bridge. From the white side, of course.

I was looking through my camera lens ready to snap the perfect picture when I noticed Moses walking onto the bridge. I yelled, "Moses, it's me—" But before I could say my name, I heard Donna Sue's voice from behind. Right away I noticed that feeling deep inside that made me wish I could disappear so I wouldn't I have to hear another word coming from her mouth.

"Did I, by any chance, hear you talking to that colored boy on the bridge?" Donna Sue yelled. "If my parents ever caught me doing that, why I'd be in the worst trouble of my life."

Her Bobbsey Twin follow-along friend chimed in, "Mine, too."

Then they marched off, just like that, before I could give them a piece of my mind. But it didn't matter because I probably wouldn't have said anything I really wanted to say.

One good thing: I did muster up enough courage to stick out my tongue.

One not-so-good thing: They didn't see me doing it. So I guess that doesn't count.

I couldn't help but notice as I watched them disappear, that they were wearing Girl Scout uniforms with ribbons and badges and matching green berets. I imagined how I might feel if I were wearing a Girl Scout uniform and allowed to attend meetings in the First Baptist Church. But that has never happened. No one has ever asked me to join a troop, probably because I'm Jewish. And of course Jews aren't welcome in the First Baptist Church here in Tipton, Mississippi, anyway.

After the Picnic

I sat in the back seat all by myself on the way home, the same as I did on the way to the picnic, wishing Pearlie May were by my side.

I wished we'd been holding the picnic basket together, hand over hand, like every year before this one.

I wished I could have whispered in her ear right then and there, "It's hard being different and being the ONLY one who isn't like everybody else."

But I couldn't.

13

My Hero

Sunday, July 5

Pearlie May used to say that when something very important happened to you, it might be a good idea to let it simmer in your head and heart before you did anything else with it, just like a fine pot of fresh cooked up apples. "It makes it all the sweeter before you taste it," she'd say.

That's why I decided to wait until this morning to write about my conversation with Miss Beaumont as I was leaving the July Fourth Picnic. Well, that was the main reason. Another reason: after a whole day of being downright miserable at a picnic without Pearlie May, I was in no mood to think about anything except sleep.

Now I'm ready.

I've replayed the conversation lots of times in my mind, though actually Miss Beaumont did most of the talking.

"Essie Rose Ginsberg! You are the person I wanted to see," she began.

Before I could ask why, she started talking non-stop. "I must make certain you plan to enter the Centennial Children's Writing Contest. You are my best reader and writer, Essie Rose.

Twelve members of your class have already promised to enter. In fact two of them, Donna Sue Hicks and Mary Jo Jamison, informed me they are ready to submit their entry. They're entering as a team."

I wanted to interrupt her to say that's because Mary Jo probably doesn't have one original idea in her empty head. But I didn't get the chance, and knowing me, I wouldn't have taken it anyway. Miss Beaumont kept on talking non-stop.

"Surely, you know someone who qualifies as one of Tipton's Five Best Heroes," she said, looking me right in the eye. "Now tell me you are going to enter the contest. I expect to read your winning entry in the special edition of the *Tipton Daily Gazette*.

Miss Beaumont held my face in her hands, forcing me to look square into her horn-rimmed glasses the way she was looking into my round ones.

"Remember, I'm counting on you, Essie Rose Ginsberg. Don't let me down."

"I won't, Miss Beaumont!" I blurted out.

And that was the end of our conversation.

I did some quick thinking about what she had said. My mind couldn't come up with a single person who I thought would qualify as a Tipton Best Hero. That was, until I found myself in the back seat of our car all alone and missing Pearlie May.

Pearlie May...oh, Pearlie May....

Pearlie May. Yes, Pearlie May!

I would write about Pearlie May.

Why hadn't I thought of her sooner? She's been my best and only friend for almost six years.

She is for sure THE BEST and definitely My Hero.

I made a solemn promise to myself right in the back seat of our car. I wrote it down because it was that important.

Dear Pearlie May,

Once I discover my business, I, Essie Rose Ginsberg, will get right on with it.

I will make you proud. I will write the best 300 words I've ever written to win the Children's Centennial Writing Contest.

Signed,

Your Honest-to-Goodness Writer Best Friend

14

A Rough Draft

Monday, July 6

Miss Beaumont was smart to encourage me to attend her creative writing classes last summer. I was smart to have saved my notes.

Like, for instance, the notes about any story's three Must-Haves: a beginning, a middle and an end. Miss Beaumont said those three pieces must fit together to make a whole, like a finished puzzle. And when we write, we should always start with a rough draft. That way we can see our ideas down on paper.

I figure my contest essay is just like a story. So this is what I have so far:

The Beginning

I need a problem or a question, like maybe, WHY is Pearlie May Gibbs one of Tipton's Five Best Heroes? Here are the facts I know first-hand:

- Pearlie May is kind, helpful and wise.
- She understands how to be a good friend.
- Pearlie May always seems to know what the right thing to do is and…
- She does it, no matter what.

The Middle

No matter how long I sit here at my desk I can't figure out what I could write that would prove my facts.

The Ending

"I'm sure you will agree with me after reading this essay that Pearlie May Gibbs is one of Tipton's Five Best Heroes."

I've re-read my first draft three times. I know I can do better once I find the middle. I'm not worried because Miss Beaumont said first drafts are just beginnings.

15

Troubles

Tuesday, July 7

If only I hadn't overheard Daddy and Mama's breakfast-table talk. This is what I get for listening through the thin walls in my bedroom.

Here's how it went:

Daddy spoke first.

"Tillie, the *Tipton Daily Gazette* has an article today about colored folks considering possible use of store boycotts in Alabama. If boycotts happen in Alabama, we could eventually see one happen in Mississippi, maybe in Tipton."

Mama spoke next.

"Don't worry, Max. It's only talk. Besides, if one does happen, our customers will stay with us. We treat them so well. It's the Commerce Street merchants that will lose customers. That's the street that will have all the troubles."

"You're right, Tillie," Daddy answered. "What I'm concerned about is that it's only going to get tougher for the colored folks and for us."

Then came the worst part. Daddy said he was getting tired.

"Tillie," he told Mama, "maybe it wasn't such a good idea after all to move down South."

I heard Mama say, "Max, I understand."

I think she hugged him. But I didn't understand.

That's when I decided to skip breakfast. I wasn't the least bit hungry.

I turned myself around. I snuggled back in bed with Sophia and whispered in her ear, "Daddy better not get too tired – at least not before Pearlie May comes home."

A Promise

Wednesday, July 8

Pearlie May told me more than once that I get stuck on one thing and think too hard and too long about it. She'd grab my hand, slide my glasses up to the top of my nose and look me straight in the eye.

"Miz Essie Rose," she'd say, "you'd do better going on to something altogether different for a spell. That way what you need to pop into your pretty little pig-tailed head will find a way in."

She'd give me a hug and say, "I know what I'm talking about. All you need to do, child, is listen."

And sure enough, that's the how and the why of

my visit to Moses Brownridge came to be. I decided that visiting him was just the "something different" I needed to do.

Our friendship was new so I didn't know what to expect, but to use Wilbur's words when he first met Charlotte, "Friendship is a gamble." If he could take a gamble, so could I. Besides, with Pearlie May gone, I needed a friend right now.

So I gave Sophia Sunday a quick wish-me-good-luck hug and ran off to the Bufords, repeating over and over to myself all the way, *This gamble better pay off.*

Moses wasn't on the front porch swing, so I had to shore up enough courage to ring the doorbell, and without a plate of Mitzvah cookies in my hand.

A colored lady dressed in a gray uniform answered.

"Hello," I said. "I'm Essie Rose Ginsberg, Moses' new friend. Is he around?"

"Well, I'm his mama and he's inside, at the kitchen table practicing his harmonica. But you are welcome to come in. Follow me," she said.

That's what I did, through living and dining rooms bigger than our entire house twice over, toward the kitchen where we stopped to listen to Moses playing Pearlie May's humming tune.

"Sounds good, Son," she said. "Now you can take a break. You have a visitor."

Moses' mama left the room, and he and I had a conversation that made me wonder about the friendship risk I took.

"Hi, Moses," I piped up. "It's me, Essie."

"I know that," he said as he picked up his pencil and drew a few lines across the middle of a big sheet of drawing paper.

"What are you drawing?" I asked.

"Not telling," Moses replied.

"Well, then can I see it?"

"Not yet."

That's when I decided I'd better change the subject if I had any chance of getting his attention.

"You may be drawing, but guess what I'm doing?

"Don't know," Moses said.

"Well, then, I'll tell you. I'm writing an essay for the Centennial Children's Writing Contest, the theme being Celebrate Tipton's Five Best Heroes. For sure, I'm writing about one of the five."

"And who might that be?" Moses asked, waving his pencil in the air.

"I'll tell if you promise not to tell another person, not even your mama."

"I promise," he said.

"To be extra sure, Moses Brownridge, repeat I promise three more times."

Moses rolled his eyes. "I'll say it one more time and that's it."

I knew I'd better agree to his one more time. That's when I whispered in his ear, "It's none other than my own Pearlie May Gibbs."

Moses rolled his eyes again. "Are you crazy, girl? The minute they find out your Pearlie May is colored your writing is going to be crumpled up and thrown smack in the nearest garbage can."

"Not so," I said. "A hero is a hero and the best is the best. It's all about what's on the inside, anyway. Pearlie May said so a million times. It doesn't matter what color is on the outside – brown or white.

"Besides," I kept talking, "knowing stuff like this is what makes her the best in the first place."

"Essie, I don't care how much you think your Pearlie May is a hero, I say it won't matter one bit as long as white folks are the ones judging your writing."

He shook his head back and forth. "Why are you even doing this?"

"Because I have to, Moses Brownridge. I have to figure out my business so I can get on with it and make Pearlie May proud. And this could be my business."

Moses shook his head some more.

"Besides," I said, "Pearlie May told me sometimes a person has to own up to doing what feels right when that feeling comes from deep down in your heart and soul. Even if it's scary."

Now it was my turn to shake my head, only up and down. "Pearlie May called it 'shoring up your courage' to do the right thing. And that's what I have to do now."

Moses didn't say another word. He kept on drawing, turning his paper so I couldn't see his picture.

It was time, I figured out, to end our conversation.

But before I marched myself out, I made him a bet. "Moses," I said, "if you're right and I'm wrong, I'll give you my frozen Milky Way bar."

Thinking

Thursday, July 9

I never thought the day would come when I'd have to admit a Pearlie May idea didn't work. But taking a break and visiting Moses did nothing – not one iota – to help me with that tricky middle section of my essay.

So this time I decided to try an idea of my own.

I walked to the Catherine Lee Whitcome Public Library on W. Broad Street. The sign Miss Beaumont had put on the front door read, "You are about to enter a good place to read and a good place to think."

I did want to think, but I also needed to renew my copy of *Charlotte's Web*.

Except, am I ever lucky. Miss Beaumont said because I was her best reader and writer, she'd allow me to keep the book as long as I needed, just so I returned it before school started up in the fall. Secretly, I never want to return it, but of course I would.

Miss Beaumont stamped my library card. Then she surprised me. She offered me a chocolate cupcake with sprinkles on top.

"It's in honor of Mr. E.B. White's July birthday. Take a few minutes to read my Author's Birthday Bulletin Board. You may find a quote or two that strikes your fancy."

I did exactly what Miss Beaumont said. I read every single one. I copied down my favorite Mr. E.B. White quote which is, "Hang on to your hat! Hang on to your hope. And wind the clock, for tomorrow is another day."

They were just the cheering up words I needed to hear. And now that they are in my Writer's Notebook, I can look at them any time I want.

Before I headed home, I decided to sit down on what I named "the Pearlie May Gibbs step" to finish my cupcake and think some more on Mr. E.B. White's quote. If only I had decided to go straight home, I would have avoided hearing Donna Sue and Mary Jo bragging and I wouldn't have to write down their lopsided unfair and mean conversation.

"Essie Rose," Donna Sue said, "I want you to know why we're here. Don't you think that's a good idea, Mary Jo?"

Mary Jo nodded her head up and down. Then she said, "Yes. You tell her."

Donna Sue spouted off, "We're here to tell Miss Beaumont we're on our way back from the Post Office where we are absolutely certain we mailed the winning entry in the Centennial Children's Writing Contest. Mary Jo, I think we should tell Essie Rose who we chose."

"Me, too!"

"On the count of three...together," Donna Sue said.

I put my hands over my ears because I didn't want to hear the name, but they blurted it out anyway. Loud and clear.

"Miss Marion Bishop, our Sunday School teacher."

Then they did their usual giggling and snickering and together, like always, they pranced off into the library. I quit thinking about Mr. E.B. White's quote and started thinking about other things.

Like, for instance…

1. What it might feel like when and if I ever shore up enough courage to tell Donna Sue and Mary Jo a thing or two about how I hate the way they treat me. I've never seen them treat Billy Dexter or Jenny Long or Peggy Ann Malone or anybody else, for that matter, the way they treat me. Maybe Pearlie May is right. They could very well have some good points, except they never bother to show them to me.

2. What it might feel like to go to a real Sunday School at a real synagogue, not Daddy's Friday Night Bible School at our home.

I moped all the way home knowing Pearlie May wouldn't be there for a Thinking-On Time or more important, for a Two-Peas-in-a-Pod hug which I REALLY REALLY need.

Kitchen Table Inspiration

Friday, July 10

I started the day sitting at my desk in my pajamas holding Sophia Sunday. I re-read Mr. E.B. White's quote about hope and tomorrow being another day. But that tricky middle part of the essay was still causing me big-time problems. So I decided to take another look at those notes I'd saved from Miss Beaumont's Creative Writing class. What a lucky idea. It was the introduction notes I'd skipped that unstuck my writing.

I read Miss Beaumont's words out loud to Sophia Sunday.

"Before a writer puts pencil to paper, he or she would do well to seek out a special place where INSPIRATION might choose to weave its magic."

I closed my eyes and thought and thought.

"Sophia Sunday," I finally shouted, "let's go! I figured out my INSPIRATION place."

It was, of course, the kitchen table where I used to sit with Pearlie May every morning while she drank her cup of coffee and we had our Breakfast Bible Lesson – her version – before she started her work.

I grabbed my pencil and paper and Sophia Sunday. I propped her up in my chair, and I sat myself down in Pearlie May's chair. But the minute I did, the missing began and so did the tears.

I wondered what Pearlie May would do if she were the one sitting in this chair. Why, of course, she'd be wiping my tears and saying, "Lord a mercy, Miz Essie Rose, what's troubling you now, child?"

And I'd blurt out my worries and fears. I'd go through all of them, one by one from A to Z. She'd give me a big hug and then she'd blurt out one of her Half Dozen Words of Wisdom that she'd told me over and over were so important she had to pass them on to me.

Well, INSPIRATION struck like a flash of lightning in a Mississippi summer thunderstorm. And that's how my tricky middle part came to be.

I would use Pearlie May's words – not mine.

I pictured my essay and how it would look. Short and simple and to the point, to borrow Miss Beaumont's words.

Beginning

I nominate Pearlie May Gibbs to be One of Tipton's Five Best.

Why? Because she deserves this honor. Pearlie May lives by the words she teaches me. If all the citizens of our town practice them, we can make Tipton, Mississippi, a better place.

Middle

Here are PEARLIE MAY GIBBS' HALF DOZEN WORDS OF WISDOM, the words she lives by, as told to her by her mama as told to her by HER mama.

Number One: Don't Fret

Number Two: Be Kind

Number Three: Practice Patience

Number Four: Don't Let Wrongs Fester

Number Five: Mind Your Mouth

Number Six: Shore Up Your Courage
to Do the Right Thing

Ending

I know you will agree with me and choose to make Pearlie May Gibbs one of Tipton's Five Best Heroes.

And that's all there was to that.

I held the winning essay in one hand and Sophia in the other. Together we danced our way through the house. "Sophia, I did it!" I sang. "I figured out my business, got on with it and found the way to make Pearlie May proud."

If Charlotte were spinning words in her web for me, she might have spun, "Some Writer!" the way she spun "Some Pig!" for Wilbur.

Which reminds me. Here are three more words I added to my Charlotte the Spider Word List:

SOME PIG and HUMBLE.

A Second Letter

Saturday, July 11

First, there was Pearlie May's "I Have to Leave" letter. Now there's a second letter I wish I'd never found. But there it was on the kitchen table this morning, right next to Mama's half-empty cup of coffee.

I copied it word for word in my Notebook, hoping if I did, the words would be different from what I read the first time.

> *Dear Tillie,*
>
> *I've been reading new articles every day in our newspaper about what's happening in*

Mississippi and other places in the South. It concerns me greatly that the Ku Klux Klan seems to be on the march. I read they are actively burning crosses on the grounds of Negro churches in some places. Is this happening in Tipton? I know that the Klan targets other minorities. Unfortunately, we Jews are one of those. I worry so about you and Max and Essie Rose.

Please keep me informed of your situation. I want you to know all of you are welcome to come stay with David and me here in New York or if you wish, I will start looking for a place for the three of you. Take care.

With much affection,

Your sister Rachael

P.S. One more thought just occurred to me. In case your situation worsens quickly and you feel you must leave on short notice, David knows first-hand of a business that specializes in store liquidations all over the country.

Well, I know the meaning of thousands of words, but that was the first time I ever ran across the word "liquidation." I ran back to my room and grabbed my Webster's dictionary. I flipped through the pages until I came to the letter *L*, then I moved my shaking finger down the page until I found this: "*Liquidation...to close one's store....*"

I slammed the dictionary shut.

Then I grabbed my red pencil and wrote in big letters on a blank piece of paper:

**TROUBLESOME WORRY NUMBER TWO
DADDY WILL CLOSE HIS STORE BEFORE
PEARLIE MAY COMES HOME**

I tossed that piece of paper inside my Worry Jar, right on top of Troublesome Worry Number One.

I held Sophia Sunday tight. "I'm scared, Sophia," I whispered in her ear, "scared as Wilbur seemed to be when he heard the news that he might be killed like all the other pigs before him."

Smile

Sunday, July 12

I'm too upset today to write like I usually do. Instead, I'm choosing one of Miss Beaumont's "Write for Fun" summer exercises – Exercise Number 7, to be exact:

Write down every word you can think of that puts a smile on your face.

Here goes:

    Pearlie May Gibbs

    Orange-flavored popsicles

    Frozen Milky Way bars

    Daisies

    TERRIFIC

    Wilbur

    Charlotte

    The Catherine Lee Whitcome Public Library

    Sunshine

    Birthdays

    Red bandanas

    Sophia Sunday

    Anything purple

    My cousins Julie and Sammy

    Birthday cakes

And I'm choosing to sit on my bed and think about having a friend like Charlotte the Spider and maybe wondering if it might be Moses Brownridge.

Courtesy Note

Monday, July 13

Miss Beaumont said it's always a good idea to write a courtesy note when you're sending something important.

Today I worked on coming up with the proper words to go with my contest entry. I finished it in less than five minutes.

Dear Judges,

Thank you for taking the time to read my Centennial Children's Writing Contest Essay. I hope you will decide to make my Hero — Miss Pearlie May Gibbs — one of Tipton's Five Best.

Please take very good care of the picture that, according to your rules, I had to send with my essay. It is the only one I have of Pearlie May. I must have it back.

Sincerely,

Essie Rose Ginsberg

P.S. For good measure, I rechecked all the other contest rules. I didn't miss a single one, including using the correct number of words — no more than 300. I only used 127, to be exact. That's all the words I needed to write my honest-to-goodness best-ever writing.

My Hope

Tuesday, July 14

I've been humming Pearlie May's humming song to myself all day.

I read my essay and my courtesy note three more times just to be sure. Here's what I think of it:

I WROTE MY BEST EVER WRITING.

I GOT ON WITH MY BUSINESS ONCE I FOUND IT.

I MADE PEARLIE MAY PROUD (the best way I knew how).

I hope this is what Pearlie May meant in the letter she left me.

We are All the Same

Wednesday, July 15

Whether or not this was what Pearlie May REALLY meant by getting on with my business, it did not keep me from making sure I'd always remember the morning I mailed my winning essay. That's why I've decided to use my purple pen and my best cursive writing for today's entry.

Here's exactly what I want to remember.

First things first was getting myself ready. I dressed up in my red and white flowered sundress with the crisscrossed straps, the one that was Pearlie May's favorite. I even slipped on a pair of red socks and my white patent leather Mary Janes. I recited what I knew Pearlie May would say. "Miz Essie Rose, my, you look pretty as a picture. Those colors surely do bring out your Old Soul dark eyes."

Second things second was getting my essay ready. I found just the right size envelope. Then I sat down at my desk, took my time making sure I double-checked the address, and licked the stamp with George Washington's face on it. I tucked my masterpiece inside my backpack so the early morning dew wouldn't make it soggy.

Third things third was my walk. I sang my best friend's song, "Swing Low, Sweet Chariot" from the minute I left my house to the minute I set foot in the Tipton, Mississippi, United States Post Office.

Fourth and most important was the mailing because it was last things last. I stood in front of the slot labeled "TIPTON MAIL ONLY." The clock on the wall read 8:46 a.m. I reached inside my backpack and gently pulled out my prize-winning essay. I looked up as high as my neck would stretch, to those few wispy clouds that almost looked like smiles. I closed my eyes.

"Please God," I whispered, "make my Pearlie May essay be a Children's Centennial Writing Contest winner."

The clock on the wall read 8:48 a.m. when I

dropped into the slot the most important writing I ever wrote as an Honest-To-Goodness Writer.

Oh, and there was a fifth thing – a surprise. My unplanned trip to the library to thank Miss Beaumont for her encouragement and to let her know I'd kept my promise.

"Miss Beaumont," I said, "I'm here to tell you I mailed my Children's Centennial Essay."

"Good for you, Essie Rose. I knew my best writer would not let me down."

"Thank you for your help."

And with those words, I flew out of the Catherine Lee Whitcome Public Library. I did not want to give Miss Beaumont the chance to ask me who I'd nominated. That was a secret between me and Moses and that's how I wanted it to stay. But what happened next still makes me wonder, which is why I'm changing over to my red pen and writing in cursive.

As I was passing the Buford's important house on Magnolia Avenue, I noticed with my own eyes and nose something about their fancy mailbox. It was hidden by honeysuckle vines growing clear up the painted wooden pole. The smell from the white blossoms was so sweet I reached over to pull one of them off the vine.

"Essie, they taste real good." I heard from behind.

I looked back. It was Moses. He was carrying a small bag from Kroger's.

"I wouldn't know about that. My mama warned me honeysuckle blossoms were only to look pretty and smell delicious."

"Shucks, that's no fun," Moses said as he walked next to me. "In case you ever decide to try one, I'll show you how."

He set his grocery bag down and plucked a large blossom from the vine. He held it in one hand. With the other hand, he pinched off the tip and pulled on the silky-looking string until a drop of nectar appeared. Then he quickly licked the nectar with his tongue.

"Tastes real good, real sweet, sweeter than honey," Moses said smacking his lips. "Here," he said, picking another blossom. "Now you try it."

"Oh, all right, but only this once. I do deserve something sweet today."

"How come of that?" he asked.

"Because of what I just did where I just came from," I proudly announced. "I, Essie Rose Ginsberg, dropped off the winning Centennial Children's Writing Contest entry at the Post Office."

Moses froze like a statue.

"Essie, I already told you, you're crazy to even be thinking you got a chance at winning. No colored person is ever going to be a hero in this town."

I snapped back. "Moses Brownridge, I don't care what you say. And I told you once and I'll tell you again. Pearlie May said brown or white – it didn't make a difference because on the inside we were all the same. And, besides, she is never wrong."

"This time, Essie, don't be counting on it."

"But I am."

I marched off leaving Moses licking on another honeysuckle blossom and me feeling angry at my friend.

Why couldn't he have celebrated my special Pearlie May Post Office Day with me the way Charlotte celebrated Wilbur's special County Fair day?

Another Rough Draft

Saturday, July 18

I am not worried that an Honest-To-Goodness Writer like me skipped writing in this Writer's Notebook for two whole days. Miss Beaumont once told us taking a break might be the secret to "rekindling" one's creative energy.

I think the pictures of fancy la-di-da paintings I cut out from an old Sears & Roebuck Catalog of Mama's add some nice color to this notebook. I also like how I covered a page with traced four-leaf clovers that reminded me of the one I keep in my red-and-black checkered hat box, which is nothing I'd ever show Moses.

And time off did the trick. Today I wrote something I never ever dreamed I would be writing – my first-draft ideas for my Centennial Children's Writing Contest Acceptance Speech.

1. Thank the judges.

2. Think of a catchy line to get the attention of the audience, like the one Mr. Lurvy spoke in *Charlotte's Web* when his pig Wilbur won first prize at the County Fair. "It is deeply satisfying to win a prize in front of a lot of people."

3. Talk about why I chose Pearlie May to be a Tipton Hero.

4. Read her Half Dozen Words of Wisdom to the entire crowd.

But then I got scared just thinking about winning. Me, Essie Rose Ginsberg, the only not-so-sure-and-strong student at Robert E. Lee who never raises her hand to answer a question even when she knows the answer 100%, would be on stage looking out on a crowded football field.

That's why I scrapped #2 through #4 and added a last idea, #5.

5. Introduce Pearlie May. Give her a big hug on stage. Say a final "Thank you" and walk off with Pearlie May. Pearlie May and Essie Rose, like always, Two-Peas-in-a-Pod.

Hand-Me-Down Worries

Sunday, July 19

I love reading *Charlotte's Web* so much, I read some chapters over and over. I was just about to read Chapter 4, "Loneliness," again, when Mama knocked on my bedroom door.

"Essie, please get ready for a ride. Your daddy has one of his hunches. He wants to go past the store to make sure everything is in order."

As soon as I crawled into the back seat of the car, I closed my eyes. It was time to make a Miss Beaumont Mind Picture, for sure.

I see Pearlie May's Homecoming Celebration. Homecoming posters. One has Pearlie May's picture on it, the one from the Tipton Daily Gazette. One has words on it like, for instance, Welcome Home! And one has pictures — daisies, stars, sunflowers, and a picture of a spider web. Maybe I'll even write the word Terrific inside. I see platters of cookies and cakes on the kitchen table and a bouquet of Pearlie May's daisies in the middle.

I kept my eyes closed most of the way to the store. I wish I could have kept my ears closed, too. I wish I hadn't heard Mama say, "Don't worry, Max, just more of the same."

Same what? Maybe more words starting with the letter *J* that scared me silly.

Just for today, I wanted to leave all the worrying to Mama and Daddy. Come to think of it, I wonder if all my worrying is a hand-me-down directly from them.

P.S. My Mind Picture disappeared.

Time on the Swing

Monday, July 20

This is what I reminded myself umpteen times today: *Essie Rose Ginsberg, don't let anything stop you from getting on with your new business of planning Pearlie May's Homecoming Celebration. Not Daddy's store problems, and not Pearlie May's still being gone with only 11 more days until the Centennial. She will be home. She HAS TO.*

Lucky for me yesterday's Mind Picture came back to me this morning. I decided to make it come true.

I finished posters one and two in no time flat. But no matter how much time I spent on poster number three, I couldn't get it right. I felt a lack-of-patience hissy fit brewing after ten tries at drawing a spider web. Each one looked the same – a squiggly mess. I broke Number Three of Pearlie May's Half Dozen Words of Wisdom: Practice Patience. I scribbled over the whole page.

I am an Honest-To-Goodness Writer. I am not an Honest-To-Goodness Artist.

Except, I did know someone who was. After our last conversation, I wasn't sure that someone was my Honest-To-Goodness Friend. But I had to take a chance on Moses Brownridge or else there'd be no drawing for my poster.

Without giving it another thought, I grabbed the poster and my copy of *Charlotte's Web* so I could show Moses a picture of the spider web I needed him to draw.

Ordinarily, I would have avoided Mattie Lou. But today I showed her my best manners because I felt an Old Soul feeling warning me Pearlie May might be watching my behavior from over in Spring City.

"Mattie Lou," I said, "I'm going to visit a friend. I'll be home soon."

"Don't be gone too long," she said.

Then I waltzed off to visit Moses Brownridge. But I came to a screeching halt when I noticed something

with my own eyes. It was a sign poking up from the
ground next to the Buford's mail box.

HOUSE FOR SALE
Contact: Martha Webster
Webster & Jones Realtors
Telephone: 839-2325

"No. Not now!" I shouted, nearly dropping my
poster and book. "Not with everything else happening."

I hoped it was a mistake, a big mistake, but when I
noticed Moses sitting on the swing, I knew something
was wrong. His baseball cap was pulled down over his
face and he was twiddling his thumbs. The swing was
as still as the breezeless Mississippi summer day.

I sat down next to him. "Moses," I said, "are
you okay?"

"Not really," he answered. His voice was so quiet
I had to scoot in a little closer.

"Is what's wrong that sign I noticed next to
the mailbox?"

"Yeah," he mumbled looking down. "Mrs. Buford
took a real bad fall down the steps three nights ago.

First thing this morning, Mr. Buford told Mama he was done with this big old house. He told her it was time to get rid of it and move in with their daughter down in Alabama."

I quickly wiped the tears that I felt falling down my cheeks so Moses wouldn't notice.

"Moses, what will happen to you and your Mama?"

"Don't know yet," he said, tapping his foot. "Most likely she'll get a job for another white lady, probably in Monroe, where her sister lives. Because she's not sure when Pa will get on home, she says that will be as good a place as any for us to wait."

"I don't want you to move anywhere, Moses. I want you to stay here."

"I want to stay here, too. I'm used to this place."

Then I noticed with my own ears how everything got quiet. Real quiet. So quiet, in fact, I could hear the sound of my own breath, and Moses', too.

It was Moses and me sitting on the swing – both of us staring down at the ground and neither one knowing what to do or what to say.

All that quiet got me thinking about Daddy and the store. And that got me thinking about Pearlie May. And that got me thinking why I'd gone to visit Moses in the first place. I wondered if this was a good time to ask Moses for help with my posters. But maybe we both needed a change of thought. So I shored up some courage.

"Moses, I know this may not be the time to tell you why I came today, but I'm going to tell you anyway." And without knowing for sure if he was listening, I chatterboxed away about Pearlie May's Homecoming Celebration I was planning and the posters I'd made and the one that needed his help.

Finally I stopped and took a deep breath.

"Moses, will you help me, please?"

"Essie, sure I'll help you, but I still don't think you understand. You're wasting your time. No colored person will ever win that contest."

"Moses Brownridge, you are wrong." I jumped in, "and if you were really my friend, you wouldn't say those things."

"Essie, I am your friend. That's why I'm saying what I'm saying because I don't want you to get hurt. But, no matter, I'll help you with your poster."

"I need you to draw me some stars, daisies and sunflowers." I opened my book. "And Moses," I said while flipping through the pages, "I need you to draw this." I pointed to the web Charlotte had spun.

"Who's Charlotte, anyway?" Moses asked.

"She's the spider who saved her friend Wilbur the pig from being killed by weaving a web with special words she wrote inside it."

Come to think of it, Moses might save me with his drawing of a spider web that is so perfect, I'm certain it would make Charlotte herself proud.

27

One Good Turn

Tuesday, July 21

If I could have had a Thinking-On Time with Pearlie May about everything Moses has done for me, I know exactly what she'd say. "Miz Essie Rose, child, you know one good turn deserves another. I expect you to be your best self and figure something out, and don't wait too long to do it."

It took some figuring, but in the middle of the night I finally came up with a Return-the-Favor Plan – one I hoped would please Moses.

After breakfast, I went over to check it out with him.

"Moses," I said when his mama called him to the

front door, "I've been thinking how much help you've been to me. And like Pearlie May would say, 'One good turn deserves another.' You do your best drawing for me. I want to do my best out-loud reading for you."

Then I chatterboxed on about how Miss Beaumont had saved *Charlotte's Web* for me when I didn't know why because it was about a spider and a pig and she knew I liked books that were true. I kept on about how Charlotte and Wilbur had become my friends and how they help me when I fret about Pearlie May being gone. Come to think of it, I was talking so fast I didn't notice if Moses was listening or not.

I finally quit chatterboxing long enough to cross my fingers and pop the big question.

"Moses, would you like it if we read *Charlotte's Web* together?"

Moses nodded. "Maybe, but I'll need some time to think about it, Essie."

"Okay," I said, "but don't take too long."

On the walk home I noticed three thoughts swirling inside my head.

Thought Number One was that if we read every chapter two times, that would mean LOTS of Moses time.

Thought Number Two was how disappointed and sad I'd feel if Moses said NO to my plan.

Thought Number Three was I might have a name for my Writer's Notebook – *The Summer I Found a New Friend.*

Supposings

Wednesday, July 22

I wasn't SUPPOSED to be having all these supposings. Like, for instance, suppose what Moses said about the contest was true?

Suppose he did know more than me about the way things worked in Tipton?

Suppose he did know Pearlie May could never win because she was colored?

Suppose he did know when the judges looked at her picture, they wouldn't read my essay?

I wanted all my supposings to disappear.

I closed my eyes and made a wish:

I wish Pearlie May were here to tell me a story or sing me a bedtime song like the way Charlotte did for Wilbur when he was so tired from having to prove to his friend that he was still radiant.

29

Off the Blue Line

Thursday, July 23

I know Miss Beaumont said a Notebook is a safe place to write down any thoughts and feelings, but the ones I woke up with this morning were too scary for me to set down on this page.

In fact, it took me until bedtime to shore up the courage to write down my One Worst "Suppose I Couldn't Do Anything About It" Fear.

If I don't win the Centennial Children's Writing Contest being an Honest-to-Goodness Prize-Winning Writer, maybe writing ISN'T my business after all. And now how will I ever be able to make Pearlie May proud?

I re-read what I wrote. I noticed with my own eyes something I hated, how my pencil slipped and how every other word wasn't on the blue line.

I closed my Notebook, hugged Sophia Sunday and cried myself to sleep.

30

New Courage

Friday, July 24

I'd lost all my nerve – just the thing Charlotte had told Wilbur not to do. Between all my Moses supposings and my One Worst "Supposing I Couldn't Do Anything About It" Fear, I had zero energy left inside me to muster up an ounce of courage.

How could I get my courage back?

Since it was Shabbos, I wondered if maybe one of Daddy's Friday Night Bible Stories could do the trick. But which one? I'd heard the Moses story, the Jonah and the Whale Story, and the Noah and the Ark story so many times I had them memorized. All three stories had heroes, but what I needed tonight was a story about a heroine. That's when Esther and her story of bravery and courage came to mind, except Daddy only told that one on Purim.

I needed to hear Daddy tell me again how Esther was willing to go before the king and admit she was Jewish in order to save her people – knowing she might be killed. I needed Daddy to tell me again how brave it was of her to leave her home and family. Most of all, I needed him to tell me how Esther was able to keep up her courage.

I suppose thinking about how Esther shored up her courage to go before a king gave me enough courage to go before Daddy.

"Daddy," I said, after we'd finished saying all our Blessings, "just this once, may I please choose the Friday Night Bible Story? I know it's not Purim, but I really want to hear the Esther story again."

I was certain he'd say, "No, Essie Rose. It's not the proper time."

Instead, to my surprise, Daddy agreed. He told me the whole story of Queen Esther, from the beginning to the end when evil Haman gets what he deserves.

And that's not the only surprise of this Shabbos. There was another more amazing one.

While he was telling the story, Daddy did one of those Miss Beaumont "digressions." Only he called it "reminiscing" about the Purim Parties he used to have up North when he was my age with his cousins and how they ate so many of those funny-sounding three-corner cookies, they got belly-aches.

"Your grandmother made the best *Hamantaschen* cookies in New York," Daddy bragged.

I got to thinking how much fun it might be if we had a Purim Party, right here in Tipton.

Except who would we invite?

31

Not Quite Yet

Saturday, July 25

Miz Essie Rose, quit all this flitting around from room to room. Settle yourself down. This is as good a time as any to practice patience. Now child, you go find something to keep your pretty little self busy. It'll make waiting easier." That's what Pearlie May would say if she were here.

Well, with only six days left until the Centennial and no word from the Judges or from Pearlie May, I know one thing: I've waited long enough. Come to think of it, it's been 22 days, to be exact, since I've heard one word from Pearlie May. And 10 days, to be exact, since I've been waiting for the judges to send my winning notice.

My Old Soul self kept saying no matter what I decide to do today, it probably won't matter.

And my Old Soul self was absolutely correct.

I decided to take a walk for a change-my-mood double scoop of peppermint ice cream. The nearer I came to Latham's Rexall Drugstore, the more I wondered, *What if Donna Sue and Mary Jo are having ice cream, too, and I bump into them and they make fun of me again?*

My answer to myself surprised me. *So what if they do. This time you'll shore up your courage and tell them a thing or two.*

I prepared myself, coming up with the words I'd yell. "*Both of you need to do what Pearlie May taught me. You need to learn to mind your mouths because if you don't, I promise one day you'll be sorry and I mean real sorry. You wait and see. SO THERE.*"

I practiced saying the words over and over, at least 15 times, to be exact.

I had it all planned out until, sure enough, Donna Sue and her shadow Mary Jo walked out of the drugstore as I walked in.

"Well hello, Essie Rose," Donna Sue said. "Are you still talking to colored boys, like what you were doing at the Fourth of July picnic?"

"Yes, are you?" Mary Jo asked.

Well, I knew what I wanted to say. I'd practiced every word. I took a deep breath. I clenched my fists. I opened my mouth.

But the words didn't come out. I felt them bubbling up, but not quite far enough.

Donna Sue and Mary Jo did what they always did. They giggled and turned away.

Right then and there, on the very spot where Pearlie May used to wait for me when we'd go together for ice cream, I made this promise to myself:

ESSIE ROSE GINSBERG, THE NEXT TIME WILL BE THE TIME YOU WILL SHORE UP YOUR COURAGE TO DO THE RIGHT THING AND MAKE THE WORDS YOU WANT TO SAY COME OUT OF YOUR MOUTH, LOUD AND CLEAR.

32

Some Numbers

Sunday, July 26

Five days until the Centennial

    11 days I've been waiting to hear from the Judges

    23 days since I've heard from Pearlie May

100% out of patience

NO NEWS FROM THE JUDGES
NO NEWS FROM PEARLIE MAY
NO WRITING

33

The Same

Monday, July 27

DITTO

DITTO

DITTO

DITTO

DITTO

34

More of the Same

Tuesday, July 28

DITTO

35

Worry #3

Wednesday, July 29

Today was the very worst day of my life. EVER.

The minute Mr. Thornton, our mailman, delivered the mail, I started sifting through it.

There it was, a letter addressed to me from the Centennial Judges Committee. I tore it open, ready to read the good news that I'd won the contest.

Instead, I'm pasting in what it really said. What I'd never imagined.

Dear Miss Ginsberg,

We received your entry for the Centennial Children's Writing Contest which you will find enclosed along with the photograph of your chosen Hero. According to the rules established by the Centennial Committee, only Caucasians are eligible to attain this honor.

Yours truly,

The Judges Committee

Mr. Charles Chesterfield, Chairman

Tipton, Mississippi Centennial

One Hundred Years in the Wheel of Progress

How could this be?

I screamed.

I stomped my feet.

I jumped up and down.

I DO NOT UNDERSTAND.

When I finally pulled myself together enough to pick up the rest of the mail I'd dropped on the floor, a picture postcard slid out from behind Daddy's latest issue of Life Magazine.

It was postmarked Spring City, Mississippi. It was from Pearlie May.

"I knew it," I shouted. "Pearlie May's writing to tell me not to worry. She'll be home just in time for the Centennial."

But when I flipped the card over to the message side, it didn't say that at all. I'm pasting in the postcard too. Another message I never imagined.

Miz Essie Rose,

I can't make it home for Tipton's Big Birthday. I am so sorry, child. Things aren't going well here. I still plan to make it home for your Number 11 Birthday.

Your Pearlie May

I grabbed a piece of blank paper and I wrote in big red letters:

TROUBLESOME WORRY NUMBER THREE

PEARLIE MAY WON'T BE HOME IN TIME FOR MY 11TH BIRTHDAY

IF THAT HAPPENS, I MIGHT NOT EVER HEAR THE STORY OF HER RED BANDANA

I tossed the paper in my Worry Jar and closed it tight.

Then I wrote a note to Pearlie May apologizing for not making her proud the best and only way I knew how. But I didn't mail it because my tears smudged up the words something awful.

Pictures in Pockets

Thursday, July 30

It's not fair," I cried to Sophia Sunday.

Moses was right. The judges disqualified me. Now I had to find a way to tell them they were wrong, more wrong than I think they've ever been in all their judgings.

But first things first: I needed to take Moses his Milky Way bar. After all, a bet is a bet and a promise is a promise and a friend is a friend.

I grabbed a Milky Way bar from the freezer and headed off to visit Moses to do the right thing.

Come to think of it, maybe doing something like this was what Pearlie May meant. Would this make her proud?

Moses was sitting on the front porch swing. I heard him loud and clear. He was playing Pearlie May's humming tune. I didn't want to interrupt him even though my missing Pearlie May grew worse the longer I listened. So instead I laid the Milky Way bar by his side.

Moses stopped playing the minute he noticed it.

"What's this for, Essie?" he asked, looking it over good.

"It's for you. Remember we made a bet? And you won. I didn't win the Centennial Children's Writing Contest. You said the judges would never choose my essay."

"Essie, I'm sorry, real sorry. I know how bad you wanted to win."

"Thanks, Moses," I said, "I did want to win that contest more than anything else to make Pearlie May proud. Besides not winning, I learned more bad news. She's not coming home yet. I'm really missing her, Moses."

"I know how that feels," he said. "That's why I

always keep my Pa's picture in my pocket so when I get that missing feeling, I take out his picture. And that helps me…a whole lot."

All the way home I thought about what Moses said.

When I got home, I took my one and only picture of Pearlie May the judges sent back and put it in my pocket.

And that's where I've kept my hand this entire day, except for now.

37

A Big P.S.

Friday, July 31

I learned a thing or two today.

Settling up with Moses turned out to be a whole lot easier than settling up with those contest judges. But I was determined today would be the day I'd write them a letter. Not a mean and nasty one. Pearlie May wouldn't like that. But a straight-from-the-heart, I-know-what-I'm-talking-about one.

First I did my homework. I re-read the unfair letter the judges sent me. To be sure I understood the meaning of the word "Caucasian," I looked it up in my Webster's

Unabridged Dictionary. It means "of the white race." Then I re-read the contest rules, front and back, upside down and inside out. That one word was nowhere to be found. Then, following Miss Beaumont's advice, I organized my thoughts inside my head.

Now I was ready to write the judges an Essie Rose Ginsberg letter they'd never forget.

Here is what I wrote:

Dear Mr. Chesterfield and all the other Judges,

I am writing to tell you your rule that "Caucasians only are eligible to win the contest" is not fair. I re-read the Centennial Children's Writing Contest rules three times — every single word. And I couldn't find that word "CAUCASIAN" anywhere. Besides, even if it were mentioned, Pearlie May Gibbs says it makes no difference what color a person is on the outside. It's what's on the inside that counts.

No matter what you and your rules say, I know Pearlie May Gibbs is and will always be my Hero and she has all the qualifications to be one of Tipton's Five Best.

I will find another way to make certain Tipton, Mississippi, knows about my Pearlie May Gibbs and her Half Dozen Words of Wisdom because they are that important. You wait and see.

Yours truly,

Essie Rose Ginsberg

P.S. (A Big P.S.) What kind of progress do you think you've made here in Tipton, Mississippi, by not making Pearlie May a hometown Hero because she's not Caucasian?

I folded the letter, put it inside an envelope and marched myself right then and there, just as I was, off to the Post Office. I didn't want to lose whatever courage I'd shored up.

I dropped my letter into the very same slot I'd used for my essay. Only today I wasn't celebrating.

I walked toward home, but home was not where I wanted to be. I wanted to be at the Catherine Lee

Whitcome Public Library. So I changed direction.

The minute I walked in, Miss Beaumont noticed me.

"Essie Rose, I'm about to take down this month's Author's Birthday Bulletin Board. It is the last day of the month, you know. Would you like to help?"

"Sure, Miss Beaumont," I answered.

"Pick any quote from E.B. White on the board. You may keep it if you like."

Here's the one I picked: "A library is a good place to go when you feel unhappy, for there in a book, you may find encouragement and comfort."

I stayed in the Catherine Lee Whitcome Public Library until Miss Beaumont tapped me on the shoulder. "Essie Rose," she whispered, "it's five o'clock. Time to close the library."

I followed Miss Beaumont out the door wishing with all my heart Pearlie May would be waiting for me on her step.

But she wasn't.

38

Centennial Day One

Saturday, August 1

The only way I could think of to make it through Day One of the Centennial without Pearlie May was to practice being an Honest-to-Goodness Writer who could write anything, anytime, anywhere. So I walked around listing sounds I heard with my own ears and sights I saw with my own eyes. And NOT doing a Pearlie May No-No, which was fretting. It was also good practice for describing.

What I Saw

1. Boys and girls eating cotton candy and caramel apples on a stick
2. Men and women, boys and girls prancing around in olden time costumes
3. Signs waving everywhere that read "Congratulations Tipton, Mississippi, 1853-1953."
4. Boy Scouts and Girl Scouts in their full uniforms handing out red, white and blue balloons.

What I Heard

1. The Tipton High School Band playing John Philip Sousa's *King Cotton March* (according to the program)
2. Men standing in booths shouting, "Get your hot dogs and cold drinks here!"
3. Men and women and children shouting and clapping as they watched the 30 floats move slowly down Commerce Street
4. Horns blowing

I also made one more list.

All the Things I Didn't Do

1. I didn't ride the Ferris Wheel (or any ride, for that matter)
2. I didn't play any of the games, even my favorite – Guess How Many Jellybeans Are in the Jar
3. I didn't eat any cotton candy
4. I didn't walk around Tipton's Town Square

All because Pearlie May was not with me.

39

Centennial Day Two

Sunday, August 2

Daddy insisted we arrive at the Tipton High School Football Field early today to get a "choice" parking place and a "choice" seat. He was certain the whole town – all 7,450 people – would turn out for Governor Hugh White's speech, the awards ceremony, and especially for the Fireworks Finale Extravaganza.

I knew Day Two would be worse than Day One, so I counted on my Writer's Notebook to help me through again. Especially when it came time for the unfair awards ceremony.

"Pay attention to the speech, Essie Rose!" Daddy yelled in my ear. But the football field was so noisy with the High School Band marching across the grass spelling out T-I-P-T-O-N, I barely heard a word the governor said.

Besides, I didn't care one iota about the speech or who was making it. I cared only about making sure I didn't throw a full-blown hissy fit when Mr. Chesterfield announced the winners of the Centennial Children's Writing Contest. That would be a dead giveaway for possible trouble with Daddy and Mama asking me questions. Like, for instance, "Essie Rose Ginsberg, what in the world has gotten into you?"

I reminded myself this was absolutely NOT the time or place to clue them in on what I'd done. No way. NEVER. But since I didn't win, it didn't matter anyway.

The only way I was able to keep calm when Mr. Chesterfield announced the winners was by writing in my Writer's Notebook.

When Mr. Chesterfield shouted, "Billy Dexter and your Hero, Police Officer Mr. Doug Jones," I scribbled *WHAT?*

And when he shouted, "Jenny Long and your

Hero, History teacher Mr. Dan Wilder," I scribbled *NO WAY.*

And when he shouted, "Wayne Harper, Jr. and your Hero, Fire Chief Mr. George Kentworth," I scribbled *OH BROTHER.*

I scribbled *NOT HER?* when he shouted, "Peggy Ann Malone and your Hero, School Librarian Miss Irene Billings."

The worst was when he announced, "Donna Sue Hicks and Mary Jo Jamison and your Hero, Sunday School teacher Miss Marion Bishop."

I broke my pencil scribbling *GOODY TWO SHOES TIMES TWO.*

For a minute I thought I was back in first grade Social Studies class the day we learned about community helpers. Every winner was a community helper. They all picked "proper people," according to the judges who obviously didn't think Pearlie May was a "proper" person."

I shut my Notebook and tucked it inside my backpack.

In fact, if I hadn't shut it at that very second, I would have drawn a big fat *X* from top to bottom across this Day Two of the Centennial page.

I watched the Fireworks Finale Extravaganza until the last firecracker fizzled on the ground because that's what Daddy and Mama wanted.

The Centennial was over, but my missing Pearlie May was not. Neither was my feeling sad that I didn't make her proud.

Riding home in the back seat of Daddy's car all by myself, I thought about another something I DO NOT UNDERSTAND. It seems to me the Goody Two Shoes girls were exactly like Templeton the rat in *Charlotte's Web* – always doing the right thing for the wrong reason.

I did the right thing for all the right reasons and it didn't matter, not one bit.

40

Twirling Worries

Monday, August 3

According to Mama's Kroger "Flowers of Mississippi" calendar, it's three days into my birthday month. If this year was like last year, Pearlie May and I would be having one Thinking-On Time after another about my August 16th Number 11 Birthday. We'd be sitting at the kitchen table laughing and talking and figuring out my cake and how she might fancy it up.

Instead, I'm having a by-myself-at-my-desk Thinking-On Time about a million Pearlie May worries that are making me twirl my hair nonstop. Writing them down might help.

Pearlie May Worries

1. Was Pearlie May keeping something from me?
2. How come her post card didn't say she loved me?
3. Could she be sick herself, maybe from taking care of her sister Flora Belle?
4. When exactly will she be home?
5. Will she think I'm ready to hear the story of her red bandana?

Mama and Daddy Worries

1. What if they ever find out I entered the Centennial Children's Writing Contest?
2. I heard Daddy tell Mama that Mr. Chesterfield acted "different" toward him at the Centennial. What does that mean?
3. Mama and Daddy keep having private phone calls and conversations. Will they ever tell me what's really happening in our family?

Worries about Me

1. Will I ever be strong and sure enough to tell Donna Sue and Mary Jo exactly how I feel?
2. Will I ever think of a name for this summer's Notebook?

3. Will I ever find a way to keep my promise to the judges to make Pearlie May a Tipton Best Hero, my way?

I don't even know which of all these worries is troublesome enough it needs to go into my Worry Jar. I've got to stop twirling my hair.

On the Step

Tuesday, August 4

Hallelujah! I had a just-in-the-nick-of-time surprise today when I needed one the most – an unexpected visitor bringing unexpected good news.

When I heard three quick knocks on the kitchen door, I knew it couldn't be anyone but Moses.

"I'll be right there," I shouted from my room.

"Moses," I asked, "What brings you to my house today?"

"I need to settle up on something. That's what brought me over here."

I asked Moses to come inside, but he said the

kitchen step was a fine place to say what he needed to say.

"And what is it you need to say?" I asked as we took our seats.

"Here," he said. He reached into his pocket. "I came to return that Milky Way bar you gave me because of the bet we made. It doesn't feel right, my keeping it."

I was about to tell Moses the Milky Way bar belonged to him, fair and square, but he interrupted me.

"Besides…" he said.

"Besides what, Moses?"

"Besides, I needed to get away from the Bufords. Too much is going on with all that house-selling stuff. And one more thing, Essie. You remember that return-the-favor idea you asked me to think about? Well, I thought on it. That spider and pig? They won't leave my mind."

Moses finally stopped his chatterboxing so I could start mine.

"Moses, I'm in the same boat as you. I didn't win the contest. I don't know when Pearlie May's coming home. My Number 11 Birthday is coming up in two weeks. Worst of all, I still don't know my business, so I can't make Pearlie May proud."

Then I had a thought. Moses and I were our own Two-Peas-in-a-Pod. We both needed some big time cheering up, and I had the perfect cheering-up solution.

"Moses, wait right here on this step. Don't move a muscle. I'll be right back."

I ran to my room to get something. Then I ran back to the kitchen step and parked myself next to Moses.

"Moses Brownridge, what if we spend this morning and every morning after in this very spot reading about Charlotte and Wilbur. We'll read *Charlotte's Web* from cover to cover once and maybe once again."

Moses didn't hesitate a second.

"Sounds good to me, Essie. Real good."

And that's how it came to be that the two of us sat on my kitchen step this morning reading *Charlotte's Web*.

Jacks

Wednesday, August 5

Today, Moses and I read Chapter VII, "Bad News," through Chapter XII, "The Miracle." Like yesterday, I did all the out-loud reading and Moses did all the listening.

I offered him the chance to read, but he said he liked listening better. And without my even asking him why, Moses chatterboxed about how when he looks at a page in a book, the words just jump around and sometimes they even bunch together.

I didn't want Moses to feel bad, so I decided I'd be the out-loud reader from now on.

Whenever I need a reading-out-loud break, we play a game. Today we played four rounds of Jacks. We each won two.

When Moses went home, my cheered-up feeling went along with him.

This afternoon I wrote Pearlie May a second come-home letter. I know I'll never mail it because I don't want her to know I am doubting her promise keeping. And she always knows what I'm thinking anyway. But I still needed to write it. I hoped writing it might make me feel a tiny bit better. But it didn't.

Dear Pearlie May,

I know you already know this, but my Number 11 Birthday is coming up in the same number of days. You promised you'd be home. We need to be thinking about my cake. I know you have to take care of your sister Flora Belle, but I need you, too. We always make my birthday cake together, and that can never change. Besides, this is the year I'm certain I'm ready to hear the story of your red bandana.

I miss you. I'm still trying to figure out my business so I can get on with it and make you proud. Please come home NOW.

Your Miz Essie Rose

Distractions

Thursday, August 6

Today we read all the way through to Chapter XVII, "Uncle." Every once in a while Moses would interrupt me and ask me to go back and read a sentence over. Like, for instance, the sentence when Wilbur asked Charlotte to sing him a bedtime song. I didn't ask why, but I wondered if Moses' pa used to sing him a bedtime song. Come to think of it, that's a sentence I read over and over, too.

By the time I needed a reading-out-loud break, we took a different kind. Today we walked to Daddy's store for some Crackerjacks, a box for each of us. Only we couldn't walk together. That would have gotten us both in big trouble. So we did the next best thing. We walked together, but on opposite sides of the street.

This is another one of those things I DO NOT UNDERSTAND.

This afternoon I needed some Forget-Everything-No-Hair-Twirling distractions. So I leafed through the Sears & Roebuck Catalog, read "The Ugly Duckling" (one of my favorite stories when I was seven because, even though it was not true, the duckling's feelings were true, just like mine), listened to Patti Page sing "How Much is That Doggie in the Window" on my record player, walked to Latham's Rexall Drugstore for a double vanilla cherry Coke float, and strolled home stopping every so often to sniff the honeysuckles. That means twice today I got my exercise walking to and from town.

One more thing I did was count the hours until tomorrow when I'd read my book to my friend again.

A Special Shabbos

Friday, August 7

Like all the other mornings, I sat on the kitchen step with my book waiting for Moses so we could pick up where we left off yesterday – Chapter XVIII, "The Cool of the Evening." Like all the other mornings, I did the reading and Moses did the listening. By the time I finished the next-to-last chapter, "A Warm Wind," I needed a real break.

"Moses," I said, "keep your finger on this page. I'll be right back with two cold Orange Crush sodas." That's when I noticed Mama's reminder note taped to the refrigerator door:

ESSIE ROSE, PLEASE READY THE KITCHEN TABLE TO GREET THE SHABBOS. THANK YOU DEAR, MAMA.

That's when I had a what-if moment. What if tonight I were to set an extra plate for my friend Moses?

"Well, Moses," I blurted out as I pushed the screen door open and handed him an Orange Crush, "you won't believe this, but I have another something special to ask you."

"What is it this time?" Moses asked, like he was dreading hearing anything I was about to say.

"Moses Brownridge, today is Friday, our Sabbath. Kind of like your Sunday Praise Day, to use Pearlie May's words."

Then without stopping to take a breath, I popped the question. "Will you please come and have Sabbath dinner with us tonight?" You are the first person I've ever invited in all the time I've been living in Tipton to have Sabbath dinner with me."

Moses rolled his eyes. He shook his head and tipped his baseball cap.

Finally, he said, "Essie, I don't know how you come up with these crazy ideas. Doing something like this as sure as I'm sitting here on your kitchen step will get me in a big heap of trouble."

"I promise. Mama and Daddy have told me a million times our Sabbath is a time to welcome guests. I've never had anyone to welcome until now.

You will be my first Sabbath guest. That is, if you say yes."

Moses stood up. "Essie, I don't know. This feels like it's something I ought not to be doing."

I stood up, too, and looked him straight in the eye. "Please, please, please," I begged. "You have to, Moses, you just have to."

I must have said enough pleases and you have tos, because Moses finally said, "Well, alright, I guess. But I wish you would stop coming up with your crazy ideas."

"Moses, I promise, it will be fine."

I went back to reading out loud but thinking about having a Sabbath guest and reading at the same time wasn't easy. I managed, though I probably skipped a word or two here and there. We took two extra breaks because I thought it was important to explain our Sabbath rituals to Moses. Like, for instance, Daddy's Friday Night Bible Stories and our Blessing prayers.

After a while, Moses announced he'd best be getting on home in case his mama needed something.

"Be back by 4 o'clock," I told him.

Moses tipped his baseball cap.

After he left, I did three things.

First, I ran into the house and hugged Sophia Sunday.

Second, I set the table and took special care to set Moses's plate right next to mine.

Third, I counted the hours until my friend would return.

When Moses came to the door promptly at 4 o'clock, I hardly recognized him. He was all dressed up in his Sunday Praise Day best.

I knew Mama and Daddy would be surprised to see Moses and me sitting on the kitchen step. And I didn't want either one to get riled up. So first things first, I introduced Moses the minute they pulled into the driveway.

"This is my friend Moses Brownridge," I said in my most polite voice. "I met him at the Bufords the day I took over their Mitzvah cookies. That's where his mama works. Ever since then we've become friends. Now we're reading buddies."

Then the most amazing thing happened. Daddy turned to Moses. "Well, young man, if you're Essie Rose's friend, then you're my friend as well. Friends are always welcome in the Ginsberg house."

"Even for Shabbos," I piped up, to my surprise.

"Yes," he said, "especially for Shabbos."

Daddy's YES made me feel like he had given me a thousand hugs all at one time.

I decided to write this part of today's entry on a separate page and name it because it was that important. I'm calling it Essie Rose Ginsberg's Best Ever Tipton Mississippi Shabbos.

Essie Rose Ginsberg's Best Ever Tipton Mississippi Shabbos

Before we sat down at the table, I whispered in Moses' ear, "Pretend it's your Sunday Praise Day and you're sitting in Church listening to your preacher, only tonight you're listening to my Daddy."

Moses fit in like he'd been to every one of our Shabbos dinners. I could tell he knew a thing or two about praying, that's for sure. He bowed his head and closed his eyes when Mama and Daddy recited their blessings. He listened when Daddy announced the subject of his Friday Night Bible Story.

Daddy said he'd tell the Moses story tonight. He said that was appropriate because of our Sabbath guest's famous name, and he wanted him to feel right at home. So Daddy told the whole story of Moses, how he started as a baby in the bulrushes and ended up leading the Jewish people out of Egypt across the Red Sea and receiving the Ten Commandments on Mt. Sinai directly from God himself.

Moses didn't fidget or move a muscle the whole time Daddy told his story. When Mama announced it was time to eat, Moses politely tasted her brisket and potatoes and her Lemon Jello, too.

Then I asked if we could be excused to finish reading *Charlotte's Web*.

Mama and Daddy both nodded.

So I turned on the carport light and Moses and I sat down on the kitchen step to read the last chapter, "A Warm Wind."

I noticed how my reading-out-loud slowed down on the very last page. Without thinking about it, I counted to five in between each word. I didn't want the book to end.

I guess Moses didn't want the book or our cheering up time to end either. He asked if I'd read the last page again. And I did.

Wilbur said he'd never forget Charlotte because she was a true friend and a good writer. Maybe someday Moses would say that about me.

Reminder

Saturday, August 8

I tore out a piece of blank paper from on old school tablet.

I wrote:

PEARLIE MAY PROMISED SHE'D BE HOME IN TIME FOR MY NUMBER 11 BIRTHDAY AND SHE ALWAYS KEEPS HER PROMISE.

I put the piece of paper in my pocket.

I took it out to read at least 50 times and that was before lunch.

46

No Words

Tuesday, August 11

For two whole days I couldn't write. My heart didn't have words.

I didn't leave my room.

I didn't get dressed.

I didn't eat the special food Mama brought me.

I only did four things:

1. I held Sophia Sunday.
2. I cried.
3. I stomped across my room.
4. I read the last two chapters of *Charlotte's Web* until I had just about every word memorized.

I hoped Charlotte's words to Wilbur when she told him she was dying would make me feel better, even a tiny bit. But they didn't.

I still don't understand.

We were in the living room doing our Sunday morning reading when I heard a loud sputtering noise. I ran to the window and noticed with my own eyes an old black pickup truck pulling up in front of our house. And I noticed something else. The driver had brown skin and so did the woman sitting next to him.

"Daddy! Mama! Quick, look outside. Pearlie May is home!" I yelled.

Only it wasn't Pearlie May. It was a woman who only looked like Pearlie May. It was, I found out when she came to the door, Pearlie May's sister, Flora Belle.

Mama and Daddy showed Flora Belle into the living room. She sat on the sofa, then asked me to come to her. She held my hand. Looking into her eyes was just like looking into Pearlie May's.

Then she spoke the saddest news I've ever heard.

"Pearlie May is gone forever, child," she said. "She nursed me until I felt better. Then one evening she just slumped over. The doctor said it was her heart."

Flora Belle reached out and tried to hug me. I just stood there.

"Before she passed, your Pearlie May made me promise to come here to hand you this envelope and box. She wanted you to have both for your Number 11 Birthday. She wanted you to promise not to open them until that day."

Flora Belle handed me a square-shaped box wrapped in brown paper. Then she reached inside her purse and handed me an envelope.

I remember Flora Belle asking for a hug back from me, and I remember what she said right before she left.

"After a spell you'll be fine, child, because that's the way your Pearlie May would want it. She'd want you to go on with your business, to go on being you, to go on being her Essie Rose."

Most of all, I remember she called me "child." Just like Pearlie May used to call me.

And I remember one more thing. I opened my Worry Jar to drop in the worry I was writing in big red letters.

TROUBLESOME WORRY NUMBER FOUR
HOW AM I GOING TO BE FINE NOW THAT
THERE IS ONLY ONE OF US?

47

Will Sophia Sunday Ever Be the Same Again?

Wednesday, August 12

Writing down Flora Belle's news actually made me feel worse, not better.

It started me thinking about the things I'd never see again with my own eyes or hear again with my own ears. Like, for instance, I'd never hear Pearlie May hum "Swing Low, Sweet Chariot." I'd never hear her "Hallelujahs" and "Amens" every morning. I'd never see her straighten her red bandana and I'd never hear the story of why she wore it every single day.

Thinking about all those NEVERS made me so

angry I did something I never dreamed I'd ever do. I grabbed my homemade doll and threw her clear across my room.

"Sophia Sunday," I screamed, "I hate you! You're not my friend anymore!"

I broke one of Pearlie May's Half Dozen Words of Wisdom – Number Five, to be exact. I did not mind my mouth. I sobbed buckets and more buckets of tears thinking that I may have forever ruined my one and only doll.

When I finally stopped crying and picked her up and held her close, I noticed she was wet and soggy. I wondered if she'd ever be the same, the way Pearlie May made her for me the year I turned five.

48

My Business

Thursday, August 13

I put the square-shaped box on my nightstand. I couldn't take my eyes off it. I sat on my bed and wondered what was inside. "Essie Rose, practice your patience," I told myself. "You only have to wait three more days."

But something else happened as I stared at the box.

I remembered what Flora Belle said to me before she left. In fact, I decided to write her words down in this Writer's Notebook because maybe they will help me.

Flora Belle said: "Pearlie May wants you to go on

with your business, to go on being you, to go on being her Essie Rose."

Being ME was my business? Me who never speaks up, who is never sure about things, who is never strong?

But Flora Belle wouldn't have lied about Pearlie May's last words.

So being ME – no matter what – was my business?

I opened my Worry Jar to find Troublesome Worry Number Four, the one I'd put in right after I heard that Pearlie May had died. I fished it out, turned it over and wrote what I'd figured out.

I KNOW HOW I AM GOING TO BE FINE NOW THAT THERE IS ONLY ONE OF US.

I AM GOING TO GET ON WITH MY BUSINESS AND KEEP BEING ME BECAUSE THAT'S WHAT PEARLIE MAY WANTS ME TO DO.

Five Amazements

Friday, August 14

I can't believe what happened today. It turned out to be my Day of Amazements. Now I am starting to understand some of the things that turned my life upside down. Like, for instance, the words "boycott" and "liquidation" and "Caucasian."

Amazement Number One had to do with Daddy's store.

It wasn't even lunchtime and Mama and Daddy both came home from the store. This had never, ever happened before. They always closed a little early on Shabbos, but never this early. Why would they close so early?

I didn't have to wonder for very long.

"Essie," Daddy called, "Come into the kitchen. We have something important to talk about with you."

For sure, my Old Soul warned me this was one of those times when I'd better do what he said.

So I sat myself down in Pearlie May's chair. I didn't move a muscle except the ones I used to twirl my hair.

I didn't expect the "something important" to begin with Mr. Chesterfield, but when I heard Daddy say that name, I figured I was in trouble with a capital *T*. I sat still as a statue and listened.

"Essie," Daddy said in a quivery voice, "this morning when I went to the bank, I met up with Mr. Chesterfield. Our conversation astounded me. I wasn't prepared to hear what he had to say."

Daddy fiddled with his watch and continued, "Mr. Chesterfield told me that I need to pay better attention to you. He told me all about how you nominated Pearlie May to be a community hero. And that you should have known better than to nominate our colored maid.

He told me I need to explain to you more carefully our Southern rules and ways."

Amazement Number Two was Daddy.

He said, "Essie, I suppose I don't understand Southern ways and rules anymore either. I want you to know Mama and I don't agree with one single word Mr. Chesterfield said."

Daddy said there were too many changes going on, like the possible boycott and Klu Klux Klan raids. And none of them fit our Jewish way of life.

Then Daddy turned to Mama. "Tillie," he said, "It's time to call Rachael. Tell her we're going to take her suggestion. It's time for us to move back up North. I want us to leave as quickly as possible. And liquidating the store is the best plan."

Amazement Number Three was our Sabbath.

"Essie," Daddy announced, "I didn't forget our Sabbath. But tonight I don't need to tell you a Friday Night Bible Story. YOU are our Friday Night Bible Story. And you are most certainly living up to the name we gave you."

"Esther?" I asked.

"Esther," Daddy said. "Like Esther from the Bible who was brave and courageous."

Amazement Number Four was a HUG from Daddy.

Daddy took my hand and held it tight. Then he gave me a hug that felt every bit as good as one of Pearlie May's.

"Essie Rose Ginsberg," he said, "Mama and I are proud of you."

Amazement Number Five was my Pearlie May Gibbs.

We were moving up North and I was glad.

But I was also glad we'd lived down South. How else would I have ever had my Two-Peas-in-a-Pod Best Friend Pearlie May?

50

One More Amazement

Saturday, August 15

I have declared *myself* to be **Amazement Number Six**. Because today I planned my Number 11 Birthday WITHOUT Pearlie May's help. It was a happy AND sad day.

I decided Moses would be my one and only guest at my first birthday party without Pearlie May and the last one I'd ever have in Tipton. So early this morning I walked over to invite him and tell him the sad news about Pearlie May.

Before I even had a chance to speak, Moses said, "Essie, I already know what happened to your Pearlie

May. News like that gets around fast at our church. I'm real sorry for you."

"Thanks, Moses," I said. "You know tomorrow is my birthday and I'm still planning to have my party because that would make Pearlie May proud. Will you be my one and only guest of honor?"

Moses nodded. "Sure, Essie. I'll be there."

"Two o'clock," I said over my shoulder as I headed home to bake my cake.

Lucky for me I thought of a way to make missing Pearlie May a little less troublesome. I'd simply pretend to give Sophia Sunday a cake baking lesson like the one Pearlie May gave me.

First I propped her up in Pearlie May's chair.

"Watch and listen as I do each step," I announced.

"Step One, crack the eggs and mix them with the sugar and butter.

"Step Two, add the flour, milk and vanilla.

"Step Three, grease the pan with Crisco."

And finally to the best and hardest part. "Step Four where we wait patiently for the cake to come out of the oven."

Sophia was not Pearlie May, but she was the only and next best company I had.

My pretending worked. Out of the oven came a Pearlie May golden brown birthday cake that needed only a bit of fancying up. That called for some serious Thinking-On before I came up with the perfect idea: I iced the cake with vanilla frosting I found in the kitchen cabinet – not the pink frosting I really wanted. Then I made a waxed paper funnel, the way Pearlie May taught me, and I wove as best as I could a spider web on top. I made sure to leave enough room for my 11 plus One-to-Grow-on candles.

Then I plopped down in Pearlie May's chair for a by-myself Old Soul Thinking-On Time.

Had I really figured out my business? Was it being me, the best me I could be? Is that really what Pearlie May meant in the letter she left me on the last day of school?

Sophia Sunday and I sat there way into the evening trying to finally figure it out. Knowing Pearlie May, she meant something important, something more important than any one thing I tried to do all summer. That's what my Old Soul mind was telling me. It was telling me Pearlie May never cared one iota about me making her proud.

I wished with all my heart she could have been here so I could have looked straight into her Old Soul eyes with my Old Soul eyes and tell her I understand now what she was up to. She knew my working hard to make HER proud would get me to see being Essie Rose was a good thing. Being Essie Rose was something I should be proud of.

Honestly, I think I was having one of Pearlie May Gibbs' AHAs! that came straight from the heart, one of her good and true and right revelations that take a long time coming. Like, for instance, almost one whole summer.

Number 11 Birthday

Sunday, August 16

My Birthday was not the Birthday it was supposed to be. That's for sure.

To begin with, I wasn't supposed to be opening Pearlie May's square-shaped box all by myself hours before my party. Which meant I also wasn't supposed to be reading Pearlie May's letter.

But I did, and I'm pasting it here in this Writer's Notebook so I'll always have it.

Miz Essie Rose, child, I know it's your Birthday because that's when I asked you to open this envelope and box. All these years you've been begging me to tell you the story behind my red bandana. All these years I've been telling you when I think you're ready. Well, I think you are ready.

It's real simple. My mama wore a red bandana. Her mama wore one and most likely her mama's mama wore one. My mama told me ever since she thought I was ready to hear her words that it's all about being proud — being proud no matter what your lot in life may be. My mama called her red bandana her "hat of courage." This red bandana reminded me who I was, who I am, and what I stand for. It reminded me to always hold my head up high.

Now, child, open your present. What was mine belongs to you now. Get on with your business and hold your head high.

Your Pearlie May

I gently took Pearlie May's bandana from the box and held it in my hands – never for a second taking my eyes off it. I walked to my mirror, looked at myself, then looked at the red bandana. I thought of Pearlie May and I smiled because if she were here I know what she'd say. "Child, this is yours forever, no rush to wear it. You will know when it's the right time to place it on your now 11-year-old going-on-20 head." So I decided to tuck it back in the box and keep it a secret for now.

I sat for a minute holding Sophia Sunday. I heard Pearlie May say, "No sadness. Now go out there and enjoy your Number 11 party, child."

So that's just what I did. But if I told the whole truth, sometimes I had to work really hard to keep the missing from getting in the way.

The party went like this:

Mama surprised me by decorating the kitchen table with a purple paper tablecloth. She even brought out matching paper plates and cups and birthday hats for Moses and me. Then she placed my spider-web cake smack in the middle of the table.

Moses arrived at 2 o'clock sharp. He was all dressed up in his Sunday best like what he wore when he came to our Shabbos dinner.

"Happy Birthday, Essie Rose. This is for you." And Moses handed me his present.

"Thank you, Moses," I said. "I am so happy you came."

I opened my presents one at a time:

First, Mama and Daddy's: a purple suitcase. Just what I needed for our move.

Second, Aunt Rachael and Uncle David's: a bookstore coupon to use when I arrive up North. It didn't take but a second to know I'll be buying my very own copy of *Charlotte's Web*.

And third, because I wanted to save Moses's gift for last: his was the biggest surprise of all. I couldn't believe my eyes. He'd drawn me a picture of Pearlie May wearing her red bandana just the way I'd described her.

"Oh, Moses," I said, "this is the best present you could have ever given me. This was the picture you didn't want to show me when I was visiting you, wasn't it."

I'd still be staring at the picture if Mama hadn't said, "You two, let's keep this party going."

That's when she lit the candles on my cake. They sang the Happy Birthday song to me, and Daddy quick took a picture of Moses and me with the candles all lit.

I blew out the candles and made my wish. It was the last birthday wish I'd ever make in Mississippi. Except this year, I didn't write that wish into my Writer's Notebook.

That wish belongs in my heart, so that's right where it's staying.

A Promise Kept

Monday, August 17

It's all set. Our family's last day in Tipton, Mississippi, will be on August 21st. Four days from now.

Daddy worked at the store with the liquidators all day today. Mama started packing our house.

I got started on my own packing and making my Things-to-Take-in-the-Car list. I got as far as Sophia Sunday, of course, and my red-and-black checkered hat box. But then I realized I had some important unfinished business.

Number one, I'm still taking pictures of my favorite Tipton places to put in my Mississippi Scrapbook.

Number two, I still need a name for this Writer's Notebook.

Number three, most important of all, I hadn't figured out how to keep my promise to the judges to make Pearlie May a Tipton Hero – my way.

Then out of the blue, I remembered something Miss Beaumont told me the day she gave me my first Writer's Notebook. "At the end of each summer, re-read your notebook, Essie Rose. You might get a surprise or two."

I stopped everything and began re-reading my words all the way back to that awful last day of school in June.

Before I knew it, I had a way to keep my promise.

I'd make a book, a real book, a Pearlie May Gibbs book.

I closed my eyes so I could make a Mind Picture.

I'd use my brand-new red composition notebook I was planning on saving for next summer.

I'd write a beautiful title page with the words PEARLIE MAY GIBBS' HALF DOZEN WORDS OF WISDOM, As Told to Her by Her Mama as Told to Her by HER Mama, as Written Down by Essie Rose Ginsberg.

Then I'd write her words of wisdom in purple because more than once I remember Pearlie May saying, "Purple is my color. When I feast my eyes on it, I get that uplifting proud feeling like when I'm in church on my Praise Day, singing in the choir."

Then I'd give each of her Half Dozen Words of Wisdom its own page because each one is that important.

In between I'd write some of my own words of wisdom, like, for instance, "Think on this" or "Try your best to be strong and sure."

I'd find a place, maybe at the beginning, to write a special message.

Dear Reader,

This is a very special book about a very special person. PLEASE DO NOT REMOVE IT FROM THE LIBRARY.

I closed my eyes again trying to remember every nook and corner and shelf in the library. I need to find the perfect place for my Pearlie May book.

Just Imagine

Tuesday, August 18

I still haven't figured out the perfect place for my Pearlie May book. But one thing's for sure. It is perfect.

PEARLIE MAY GIBBS' HALF DOZEN WORDS OF WISDOM, As Told to Her by Her Mama as Told to Her by HER Mama, as Written Down by Essie Rose Ginsberg looks just like yesterday's Mind Picture.

It took me every hour of this rainy day with only one break to finish the book. But it was worth it.

Whenever I got tired and wanted to stop, I held my red bandana and thought about Mr. Chesterfield and the rest of those judges and imagined their faces seeing Pearlie May Gibbs in Tipton's Catherine Lee Whitcome Public Library.

54

#2 Pencils

Wednesday, August 19

Once the sun came out this morning, I started a new roll of film and did the best I could taking pictures of Tipton for my Mississippi scrapbook.

I started with our house here on Calhoun St. and the backyard clothesline and just kept on going.

To Pearlie May's daisies. Snapped a picture.

To the Ritz Theatre. Snapped a picture.

To Woolworth's. Snapped a picture.

Some people looked at me funny, like when I took a picture of my vanilla ice cream float at Latham's Rexall

Drugstore and the Robert E. Lee School monkey bars and the GM&O train tracks that split the two sides of Tipton.

One person who didn't look at me funny was Moses. He understood exactly why I needed to remember the Buford's honeysuckles.

I surprised Moses when I gave him a goodbye present. I'd filled the burlap pencil bag that Pearlie May had made for me with 20 sharpened #2 pencils.

Moses' eyes lit up and he smiled the biggest smile I'd ever seen him smile.

"I promise to take good care of these, Essie," he said. Then he turned away and stared at all the boxes lined up on the Buford's porch and lawn. "Mama and I will be leaving soon."

"Us too," I told him, "on Friday afternoon. We're moving back up North."

Then all of a sudden I ran out of words, and so did Moses. I was blinking and swallowing so hard, the only words that I could make come out of my mouth were, "Good-bye, Moses Brownridge, I'm going to miss you."

The only ones that came out of his mouth were, "Good-bye Essie Rose Ginsberg, I'm going to miss you, too."

I turned away thinking how happy I was that Daddy had taken that picture of Moses and me with my birthday cake. It will be tucked away inside my red-and-black checkered hat box which I plan to carry on my lap the whole way to New York.

55

Jingle

Thursday, August 20

All day while we packed I kept saying the words MISSISSIPPI and NEW YORK and switching around the order. They sounded like a jingle for jumping Double Dutch.

I wonder if Donna Sue and Mary Jo ever created their own jingle.

MISSissippi **NEW** York

NEW York **MISS**issippi

Here. There.

To. From.

Up. Down.

North. South.

MISSissippi **NEW** York

NEW York **MISS**issippi

56

The Last Word

Friday, August 21

These are this Notebook's last pages I'm writing today.

My last day ever in Tipton, Mississippi.

My very last chance to place Pearlie May's book in a special place inside the Catherine Lee Whitcome Public Library.

I was ready before Daddy ever knocked to wake me. And so was my backpack. Inside I'd put the copy of *Charlotte's Web* I was returning, the Thank You note I wrote Miss Beaumont, Pearlie May's book, and this Writer's Notebook.

The time was right. I tied my red bandana just the way Pearlie May tied hers because in between my tiredness and everything else, I'd figured it out.

"I need to do one last thing," I yelled to Mama, and off I went all the way to my favorite building, the one I would miss the most.

I'd thought it all out, finally, just where in the library I should put my Pearlie May's book.

When I got there, first I placed *Charlotte's Web* in the Return Books Here basket. I left my Thank You note sticking out the side, where Miss Beaumont would be sure to see it.

Then I walked over to the Local History section. Right next to *How the Town of Tipton Got its Name*, I displayed *Pearlie May Gibbs' Half Dozen Words of Wisdom*.

There couldn't have been a more special place for a more special book about a more special person.

My mission accomplished, I walked out the library door for the very last time. But I wasn't ready to go home yet. I needed to finish one more piece of business.

I turned around and sat myself down on the very step where Pearlie May used to wait for me because she wasn't allowed to go inside. Then I reached into my backpack and pulled out this Writer's Notebook. I was finally ready to give it a title.

Even though it was almost three whole months coming, thanks to Pearlie May I'd had a Hallelujah AHA! straight from the heart.

I decided to name this Writer's Notebook *Essie Rose's Revelation Summer*. Because that is exactly what it was.

I was just about home, not even one block away, when who came prancing toward me with their roller skates over their shoulders but Donna Sue and Mary Jo.

They both took one look at me and gasped.

"Whatever IS that thing you're wearing on your head?" Donna Sue asked.

Mary Jo followed. "What IS that thing?"

I took a deep breath. I stood up straight and tall with my head held high. I waited until Donna Sue Hicks and Mary Jo Jamison were close enough so I could look both of them straight in their eyes.

It was the last time ever I'd have to face them. But for the first time ever, I was ready.

My voice was as strong and sure as I am now. My right words bubbled all the way up.

"It's my red bandana," I said, and I gave it a tug.

"Isn't it beautiful? It was a birthday present from one of Tipton's Five Best Heroes."

If a comment was coming, I wasn't waiting around. I no longer cared, not one iota. I was taking my Old Soul someplace new to be the best Essie Rose I could be.

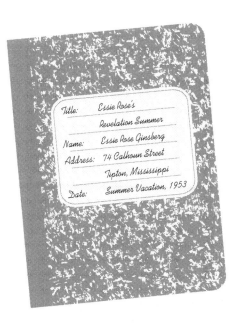

Title: Essie Rose's
               Revelation Summer
Name: Essie Rose Ginsberg
Address: 74 Calhoun Street
               Tipton, Mississippi
Date: Summer Vacation, 1953

Acknowledgements

The seeds of my story were planted in my childhood, but it took a group of devoted people, my "Assembly of Book Angels," to encourage and support me during the ups and downs of writing. To you all, in the words of Pearlie May Gibbs, I say, "Hallelujah and Amen."

Thank you to Nancy Sayre, my publisher and editor, whose words, "I love this wonderful story" changed the course of my writing life, and to Michael Sayre for his meticulously crafted and creative book design.

To Esther Hershenhorn, my teacher, my mentor, and my dear friend, thank you for declaring me a writer before I really knew what that word meant, and for telling me that "those who take leaps of faith have angels at the other end to catch them." Monna Israel, thank you for embracing Essie Rose and her story from day one, and for your countless hours of listening, encouraging, and sharing your social worker's keen understanding and sensitivity. To Carrie Barnes, my Mississippi friend, I offer my gratitude for your insights and for making certain that my facts, language, and tone were all consistent with 1950s Mississippi, the time in history depicted in the book.

Thank you to Efrain Gonzalez for the comfort of a kindred spirit, to Aaron Levine for sharing his knowledge of Jewish customs and rituals, to Renee Flager for a librarian's passion for this story, to Marlene Czarnowski for cheering me on from the beginning, and to Rob Steuer for his beyond-expectations technical support. And to Annie-Laurie, April, Janet, Karen, Robin, Sam, Tobie, Mary, Dorothy, and my family and friends who offered suggestions, confirmed ideas, read my story, and spoke these words over and over: "Never give up." To you I offer my love and appreciation.

Finally, a very special tribute to my beloved husband, Mel, who believed in me and lived through both productive and not-so-productive writing days with patience, humor, and grace. You unselfishly gave me the gift of time and space to complete this book. For your sacrifices and generosity in every way imaginable, thank you. I love you.

About the Author

Deanie Yasner writes stories that children love to read – over, and over, and over.

An author of extraordinary depth and sensitivity, she draws inspiration from her early years as a member of the only Jewish family in a small Mississippi town in the Jim Crow South. After a successful career as a special education teacher and behavior consultant, Deanie began pouring the insights she gained into stories for children.

When she is not writing, Deanie spends her time playing Scrabble, practicing Tai Chi, and daydreaming. She and her husband live in historic New Hope, Pennsylvania.

Deanie loves connecting with her readers. You can find her here:

> https://www.deanieyasner.com
> deanie.yasner@goldenalleypress.com
> https://www.goldenalleypress.com/deanie-yasner

Made in the USA
Lexington, KY
10 December 2019